Buket Uzuner

Istanbul Blues

Translated by
Pelin Arıner & Bahar Yıldırım Çotur

Milet Publishing
Smallfields Cottage, Cox Green
Rudgwick, Horsham, West Sussex
RH12 3DE England
info@milet.com
www.milet.com
www.milet.co.uk

First English edition published by Milet Publishing in 2013

ISBN 978 1 84059 852 0

"Why Doesn't Santa Love Me, Daddy?" first published
in German as "Noel Baba" in *der Freitag* (2007)

Book design by Christangelos Seferiadis
Printed and bound in Turkey by Ertem Matbaası

BIOGRAPHIES OF AUTHOR AND TRANSLATORS

Buket Uzuner was born in Ankara, Turkey in 1955. She trained as a biologist and environmental scientist, studying and working at universities in Turkey, Norway, Finland and the United States. She is a prolific and award-winning writer of short stories, travelogues and novels. Her books have been on Turkey's national bestseller lists since 1992. Her novel *Balık İzlerinin Sesi* (*The Sound of Fishsteps*) won the prestigious Yunus Nadi Prize in 1993, and her novel *Kumral Ada–Mavi Tuna* (*Mediterranean Waltz*) was named the Best Novel of 1998 by the University of Istanbul. Uzuner's books have been translated into eleven languages. A collection of her short stories, *A Cup of Turkish Coffee* (2001), was published in dual language Turkish–English by Milet, and her story "Frau Adler and the Berlin Train" was published in English translation in *Europe in Women's Short Stories from Turkey* (2012), also by Milet. An honorary member of the International Writing Program at the University of Iowa, Uzuner is a featured author at literary festivals around the world. She was selected as one of the 75 Most Influential Women of the Republic of Turkey as part of the country's 75th anniversary celebration.

Pelin Arıner was born in Turkey and grew up all over the world. She is the translator of Buket Uzuner's previous novels: *The Sound of Fishsteps*, *Mediterranean Waltz* and *The Long White Cloud–Gallipoli*. She holds an MFA in Poetry from Cornell University and has been published in *Folio, Essays and Fictions*, and *Columbia: A Journal of Literature and Art*. She lives and teaches in Lille, France.

Bahar Yıldırım Çotur was born in 1977 in Izmir and graduated from the Department of Translation and Interpreting Studies, Bosphorus University, Istanbul in 1999. She finished her M.A.S. in Interpreter

Training at the University of Geneva, Switzerland in 2007. She works as a conference interpreter, translator and part-time lecturer in Istanbul. She is an active member of the International Association of Conference Interpreters and the Conference Interpreters Association of Turkey.

EDITORIAL NOTES

Throughout the stories in this collection, we have retained the Turkish for several types of terms, including personal names, honorifics, place names and foods, among others. We have used the English spelling of Istanbul, rather than its Turkish spelling, İstanbul, because the English version is so commonly known. For the Turkish terms and other foreign language terms, we have used italics in their first instance in each story and then normal text for subsequent instances in the story. We have not italicized the Turkish honorifics that form part of a name, to avoid splitting the name visually with a style change.

TURKISH HONORIFICS

Turkish honorifics that appear in the stories and which may be unfamiliar are shown below, with their meanings.

Abla: Older sister, also used as an honorific for women.

Efendi: A title of courtesy, equivalent to the English "sir," literally meaning lord or master.

GUIDE TO TURKISH PRONUNCIATION

Turkish letters that appear in the stories and which may be unfamiliar are shown below, with a guide to their pronunciation.

c   as *j* in *just*

ç   as *ch* in *child*

ğ   silent letter that lengthens the preceding vowel

ı   as *a* in *along*

ö   as German *ö* in *Köln*, or French *œ* in *œuf*

ş   as *sh* in *ship*

ü   as German *ü* in *fünf*, or French *u* in *tu*

CONTENTS

The Sun-Eating Gypsy

There isn't a boy in the world who, having once seen a bike, does not want one of his own. I didn't. Since I could not even conceive of another living creature to take the place of my gentle, doe-eyed mule, the idea of evenings spent riding along the bank of the stream on a mechanical gadget was awfully intimidating. For days, the bike stood in our yard like a foreign object. A hostile creature! One that threatened to take my best friend, that most stubborn of the world's beauties, my mule, away from me. I told my mother I could not love anything that did not have eyes. I said I could tell whether or not a creature was good, kind and loving by looking into its eyes; but the bike did not have any. My mother gazed at me and smiled wearily. "How do you see the eyes of ants, Oğuz?" I was taken aback. Baffled. I did like ants. I got all confused and piped down.

I still don't know how to ride a bike.

Kids who grow up fatherless don't know what it's like to count on their dads during fights. I was one of them. When I got beaten up, the thing that hurt most was my lack of a father. Anger and sorrow would flare up inside me and burn like a red-hot iron. When I cried, my tears gave off the sickening smell of water sizzling on a hot grate. The smell permeated my shirts and could only be extracted if they were boiled clean. To this day, extreme sadness makes me perspire with the same odor. In such times, I would skulk off to my secret spot by the water and cry, certain that no one could see me. If a six-year-old child first discovers his personal life on the banks of a stream, he will forever remain close to nature. I would sit crying on the bank and race twigs in the water. One twig would be the good guy, and the other the bad guy. On the days I got beaten up, the bad twig would beat the good one and win.

When I got home, my mother could tell more from my sorrow-soaked shirt than from my bruises that I had been in a fight. My mother was a midwife. She was beautiful. She was twice as beautiful as any other mother. For she was both my mother and my father. She used to put me in the saddle and travel to villages on horseback for births. She was brave, she was hard working. I never knew when she was troubled or depressed, when she despaired. She always wore a tired but patient expression. She listened to all my tales of flying horses, talking streams, men who swallowed their own tongues and grass that tore its hair out, and humored them. My mother regarded, loved and raised me as a mother humors her strange son.

Once circumcised, boys begin to differ in personality from girls, their sexual identity having been clearly established for the first time. The villagers had arranged a great feast to celebrate the circumcision of their beloved midwife Seniha's orphaned son. A flutter of excitement ran through the crowd when even the head district official showed up with his family. I can still see the young girls with their trays of sherbet, the old aunties in headscarves carrying stacks of cookies, and my mother beaming with pride.

The crowd, the heat, the noise, the young girls carrying trays of sherbet, drums and pipes, the crowd, the crowd . . . My body soaked in the sweat of the Aegean heat, between my legs the bandaged, painful circumcision that seemed both funny and sad at the same time, the crowd, the fervor, the banging drums, the young girls carrying trays of sherbet . . . My absolute conviction that all men had to be circumcised . . . For that is what it takes to be a man! "Oğuz has become a man at six." "Mister, are you going to circumcise my mule, too?" My mother bustling about joyfully, smiling through the perspiration . . . Her big-boned, sturdy body quivering every time someone said "If his father could see him now . . ." The heat, the beating drums, the giggling girls scurrying back and forth with their trays of sherbet . . .

The older, plump-cheeked Emine, whose father worked at a state monopoly, perching on my bedside in her white dress and taking my hand. "I'm going to ask you something, Emine Abla, but you have to promise not to tell anyone."

When she smiled, Emine became the most beautiful girl in the world. "Mom told me that before people believed in God, they worshipped the sun and idols and fire and mountains and rocks. Then the Prophet Muhammad came and destroyed the idols with his sword, and everyone believed in God." Emine nodded and squeezed my hand. "So, Emine Abla, does that mean that the sun was God when there was no God?"

The heat, the crowd, the din . . . So very hot, so very crowded, so very loud . . . Will the girls ever stop carrying those sherbet trays . . . It hurts so badly, and all I want to do is sleep, but the heat makes it impossible . . .

"Ask whatever you wish from me, my ram, my brave son, my only Oğuz."

"I want the sun, Mommy." I wonder what the sun was like when it was God. Was it shaped like an egg or an eggplant? Was its color the pale green of a stream or the thick gold of sundown? Did it flush and roll over from sadness when God took its place?

"Mooommy, I want the sun . . ."

I cried my eyes out. I wailed and whined for hours; from the heat, the crowd, and the pain. In the evening, my mother walked up to my bedside and scolded me: "You're a man now. Learn to give up things that you can't reach!"

That was the day the bike arrived at our house, a hand-me-down from the district official's son.

Kids who do not succeed in school are not stupid. School was an institution that intruded between me and the things I loved. My obstinate mule, the stream where I raced twigs, the grass on which I lay daydreaming, the sun I plotted to capture, and my mother. I could not bring myself to enjoy sitting at a desk, thinking and speaking within established bounds. I could not get used to memorizing the writing in books, accepting other people's truths . . . After I learned to read and write, I remained the laziest, most wayward kid in every class. Yet I loved to journey with the Captains Turgut and Barbaros in books that Emine gave me, to live in mountains with the Efe of Çakırca whom peddlers spoke of, and to star in the tales of "The Prophet Ali's Sword," which Imam Efendi told whenever he came to collect manure from us. I read every book I could lay my hands on, absorbent as the Aegean soil in July. But school was a chore. We moved to town so I could attend secondary school, but my attitude did not change. I dropped out during my first year of college. After that, my mother and I never discussed the matter again. By the time I turned twenty, I had learned the printing trade and Izmir had become too small for me. I took my mother and headed for Istanbul.

A beautiful woman always makes an impression, but if, on your first meeting, she happens to be at her most vibrant and uninhibited, then she is nothing less than stunning. It was April of 1960 when I came to Istanbul.* I was stunned.

There is a mechanism in the human brain that helps keep a person adjusted by blocking out sharp and painful memories. If I were to relate everything that befell me between the ages of twenty and forty-five, it would not amount to half of my childhood memories. Two marriages, poverty, one job after another, disillusionment, pain, my mother's death, and so on. With the exception of my son's birth, I can think of nothing good or exciting that happened in those long yet fleeting twenty-five years. I stashed my poems away in a drawer together with everything else: the twigs I had raced in the stream, the hours I had spent skipping class and dashing about with my mule, the trips I had taken in the saddle with my mother, my desire to own the sun, my hopes, and all my dreams. In the meantime, I went to work at the print shop and the stationery store like a serious, settled and supposedly normal man, I returned home to eat dinner with my sweet-tempered, pretty wife who spoke impeccable Turkish, chatted with a few friends in the evening, spent time with my son (who loves school), yet still felt my mother hovering above me, saying "Stop asking for things that you can't reach, Oğuz." It was only when I was reading books, only when I could breathe freely in their wide open spaces, that I could find the strength to stand up to my mother and frown.

—Stop! Keep your dreams alive. Everyone, at all ages, must have dreams. Someone who has killed their dreams is someone who is buried alive.

---

* In 1960, in the streets of Turkey's big cities, university students were demonstrating for freedom of speech and real democracy. Street fights between police and youth were intensifying.

Just as I had started thinking "ten more years of this and I'll be dead—"

—Lift your head, look, the sun is up there. Reach out your hand and take it. But remember, as long as you hold the sun in your hand, people this side of you will remain in the dark . . .

Just as I was growing used to my graying hair and glazed, weary eyes, just as I had begun practicing the mood that went with them,

—Let us walk along the stream, let the stream be the Bosphorus and the twigs be the ferryboats. Let's make them race. Let the grass that tore its hair out be the streetcars. You can be the man who swallowed his own tongue and I'll be Emine Abla.

Just as I had resigned myself to wearing the face of Businessman, Father, Husband, Friend and Trusted Mate, to wearing the long face—

—Laughter, just like tears, can be cleansing and relieving. One should take laughing and crying seriously. The same with dreams. One who does not know how to dream, to be nourished by dreams, is barren.

A twenty-six-year-old woman with raven hair. Is she beautiful? I can't say. To me, she is lovely. I don't know how she would seem to others. She paints. Images of the sun: yellow, purple, pink, green, turquoise suns . . . Dozens, hundreds, millions of suns in one picture . . . I search for the painter of these pictures, I have to find the person who created all these suns. I must. I have no choice! My friend, the owner of the gallery, points to her: "There, that's the woman."

A twenty-six-year-old, raven-haired woman. She looks you straight in the eye. Everything is clear in her face, everything is legible. Like pristine waters, you can see the very depths. Translucent. Bright as the sun.

—When I was a kid, I asked my mother for the sun as a birthday present. On my sixth birthday. I cried for hours. Yet the house was full of all kinds of presents. You know, Oğuz, I always think about people who worshipped the sun. If I worshipped anything, it would be the sun.

"I, too, was six years old, when as a circumcision gift . . ."

A twenty-six-year-old woman with raven hair.

—There is nothing that cannot be reached. It's all in your head. Never, ever limit your imagination. Take your poems out of the drawer, stretch your hand towards the sun . . ."

"The stream, the stream from my boyhood is all dried up. I visited the village last year. Everything's changed, but the stream is what really got me. Dry as a bone. I won't be able to race twigs anymore . . ."

—You have to find other streams. Each stream that dries up must lead you to another, running stream, and so on, forever . . .

A twenty-six year-old, raven-haired woman. Is she beautiful, I can't say. To me, she is lovely.

—Ants have eyes, Oğuz. Eyes only big enough for children to see. Grown-ups can't see small things without microscopes.

"I've been seeing strange things ever since I met you. There's a fortune-teller woman, a gypsy. She appears frequently in my dreams. She eats the sun for breakfast. She looks at my fortune, says I'll fall in love with a woman named Güneş, after the sun."

A twenty-six-year-old woman. Who has not slain her childhood.

"I had another muddled dream last night. My mother, just as she was when I was a boy: Seniha, the large, sturdy midwife, I introduced you to her. 'See, Mom,' I said, 'see, I've finally found the sun,' She stared. Then she got angry. 'Stop asking for things you can't reach, Oğuz!' she said, and scolded me."

A twenty-six-year-old, raven-haired woman. "I have to go now," she said. My shirts were permeated with the stench of sadness. My wife could tell I was despondent when she washed my shirts. She did not ask. My wife never asks.

The raven-haired woman packed her bags. Threw them over her shoulder. Boarded a plane, and left. Now and then she drops me a line.

I don't keep my poems stashed away anymore.

The Mysterious Passenger at the Spanish Border

It was a train journey. Four young women, tired after a night of long, intense conversation, had finally surrendered themselves to sleep and now lay stretched out on the opposing bunk beds of a sleeping car.

As the train wound its way from the snowy Alps to the balmy Mediterranean that freezing December afternoon, the various liquors, chocolates and tobacco they had produced from their backpacks had promptly been consumed and the snapshots that filled their pockets had been passed around to exaggerated acclaim.

It was a train journey.

The group of young women, whose eldest member was twenty-four, had never met until that morning. Each one spoke a different language, but they communicated in English. Three of them were students and one was a secretary.

Barely an hour had passed since the sleeping car had fallen silent. The most devoted morning sleeper among them was suddenly awakened by a soft touch. It must have been the invisible hand that guided and protected her through all her long and lonely voyages . . .

She sat up for a moment, trying to reorient herself, then looked over at the three girls sleeping in the other beds. One must have been dreaming in Japanese, the other in Spanish and the third in French. She gently rose, descended the ladder, threw on her down vest and, picking up her Walkman, left the car.

The sight that greeted her in the corridor was nothing short of stunning. She stood stock-still, afraid that the slightest movement would shatter the moment. As the train sped south, a bare winter landscape sprawled outside its windows. There was no snow in these parts, but nature had donned its winter colors. The Pyrenees were not yet in sight. A red wheel had peeked out from behind this vast horizon and begun to rise with that innocent vanity so reminiscent of youth.

"Sunrise!" she heard herself say. She was pleased to notice that for the first time in months she had thought and spoken in Turkish. A satisfied smile lit up her face.

"Wake up, quick, get up! There's something very special I want you to see. Come on, get up, you can't miss this!"

"But Mom, I'm sleeping!"

"Not anymore. Come on sleepyhead, you can't miss this, you're going to witness a wondrous beauty you can't find anywhere else in the world!"

"Mom! Please, leave me alone . . . Nooo. Go away . . . Come on, you're ruining my own wondrous beauty here . . . Mom, no, don't take the sheets . . . Oh, Mooom!"

She couldn't have been older than ten that morning. All the other guests of the summer camp at Erdek were sound asleep, except for her mother! And of course herself! It must have been around five in the morning. Determined not to give up on her morning slumber, she hugged her pillow tight and squeezed her eyes shut. But still her mother chirped away at her bedside.

Soon afterwards the two of them were on the seashore, watching the sunrise. The weather was bone-chilling and everyone else was deep in sleep . . .

"Look at the sun! See how it rises hopefully morning after morning. Look at that splendid ascent, that strong desire to emerge. Don't ever forget, this is the most beautiful sunrise in the world, right here. Even in your most desperate hour, don't forget that. Don't ever forget!"

That's her mom alright. If it isn't the sunrise it's the sunset, or dewdrops on a flower, or constellations in the sky, or the intricate wrinkles of an old woman on the street . . . Never gives you a moment's rest . . . Always finds something to get excited about, and has to share it with her daughter . . . Never a moment's rest! Sweet, sweet rest . . .

The girl shudders from the chill and closes her eyes, succumbing to drowsiness. She snuggles up to her mother and leans her head on her shoulder. Her mom wraps an arm around her and holds her tight. Just as she's about to fall asleep she is nudged awake by a strong impulse that will recur many times in her adult years. She sits up and sees the sun.

She sees the sun and she is spellbound. For the first time she notices the glory of sunrise. There, that very morning, at that age! The sun ascends, cloaked in the hues of resistance and hope. Then she looks up at her mother, who with enraptured, half-closed eyes, murmurs:

"Look at the sea, how languid it is . . . It has been tamed; it has found peace . . . Listen, all of nature is saluting the sun . . ."

What registers in her memory, what she recollects years later, is that the most beautiful sunrise belongs to Erdek, and in truth, that sunrise is no other than her mom.

"Impressive, isn't it?"

If only the train moved a bit slower . . . Turning around, she came face to face with a graying man in his forties, sporting a moustache, wire-rimmed glasses, and thick, short-cropped hair. Such encounters are common on train journeys. A comment is made, a few words are exchanged, and all is soon forgotten. Yet sometimes, on that rare occasion, you meet a person and speak a few words that you will never forget. In either case, people who meet on trains never see each other again.

This man did not look like much of an adventurer. He seemed to be more of a philosopher type. Someone who had just stepped out of a library or a research lab after hours of study, or perhaps a mathematician . . .

"I didn't mean to disturb you. I was just so glad to meet someone else who knows that the world's most beautiful sunrise happens at the Spanish border. Please excuse my impertinence!"

"Have we arrived at the Spanish border?"

The man nodded a shy yes. Then he pointed to the Walkman on the young woman's belt. "What are you listening to?"

She hadn't started the tape yet. She took it out and handed it over to her train companion at the Spanish border. *"La Traviata.* That's the Alexander Dumas story, isn't it? Opera is the wisest choice of soundtrack for long train journeys!"

The young woman, who cherished her morning sleep, was not feeling at all talkative at that hour. She turned around and went back to gazing at the sun.

"Funny, isn't it? In moments like these one wants to believe that it is the sun that is rising and the earth that is standing still. Yet in truth it's exactly the opposite. How easy it is to be deceived; how cunning the deceptions . . ."

"Philosophy or math?" the woman asked, without taking her eyes off the sun.

"Ah, I have not introduced myself. How rude of me! My name is Walter. I am a writer. I'm German, and emigrating to America. It's not really something I want to do, but," he glanced around and whispered, "you know the Nazis, they're exterminating the Jews."

"You must be joking. The Jews are old news. It's the Turks they're after now!"

"Does that mean you're . . . are you Turkish? Oh, I should've guessed! So you're fleeing the Nazis too, just like me. But you, you are so young and alone . . ."

Just then the conductor's booming voice neared, as he rang his bell and marched the corridors, making his announcement in three different languages:

"We are now approaching the Spanish border. Please return to your cars and prepare your passports! We are approaching the Spanish border. Good morning, miss! Morning, sir! It'll be a very brief passport check, no trouble at all, I assure you!"

When she returned to the sleeping car, the young woman said good morning to her friends, who were grumbling awake in various languages. She was the oldest one among them.

The Spanish border officer turned out to be a handsome young man. Upon seeing a car full of four barely woken young women, he relaxed into a playful smile and made a few jokes that were difficult to understand due to his heavy accent. He was so pleased with the giggling of the girls that even a Turkish passport could not spoil his mood. He wished all of them a merry Christmas and a delightful stay in Spain, and left. The girls were still giddily going on about how passionate and romantic Spanish men were, when there came another knock on the door.

"I beg your pardon, I was looking for a young Turkish woman."

"Walter? Were you looking for me?"

"Ah, you're here? Are you alright? They didn't do anything bad to you, did they? Nothing degrading or hurtful? I was very concerned about you," he said. His voice was weary, and he seemed anxious. "I'm getting off here. I mean, I'm running away. I cannot bear the thought of being caught during the passport check. Do you understand? To be treated like a criminal, to be humiliated . . . These are more frightful to me than death itself. Disgusting, shameful . . ."

"But, Walter, Jews are not in danger anymore."

"That does not make the least difference, mademoiselle. What matters is the damage inflicted on one's dignity. As long as the majority of people insist on acting like wild beasts and continue reproducing in droves; as long as people believe the fallacy that violence is the means to victory . . ."

The other girls, who until that point had been giving their friend suggestive looks, thinking that this man was a new lover, now looked at her with seriousness and sadness.

"I have to leave right away, mademoiselle. Here is your opera tape. I must have carried it off accidentally. I also wanted to give you these two books. My two favorite writers. I don't need to keep them any longer, since I . . . I have to go. I must leave this minute. I must put an end to this degrading flight. Farewell . . . And take care of yourself. Farewell!"

He quickly disappeared. The Turkish girl ran after him while the other three were left staring helplessly behind. But despite her effort, she could not find him. And she never saw him again. That is the nature of long train journeys . . .

"Where are we, what town is this?"

"Portbou!" her friends replied in chorus.

She looked down at the two books that had been given to her hurriedly. One was Baudelaire's *Fleurs du Mal,* and the other was the first volume of Proust's *Remembrance of Things Past.*

When the train arrived in Barcelona, the girls exchanged addresses and said goodbye to one another. So parted the four young world travelers: one headed off to Malaga to follow Picasso's tracks, another went into Barcelona to rendezvous with her lover, and a third left in search of Cervantes . . . They sent each other a few postcards, a few words, some well-wishes . . . Then on to new journeys and other traveling companions . . . They never met again. They forgot each other's names. That is the way with long train journeys . . .

She kept with great care the books that Walter gave her. Walter, whom she had met on a train from Zurich to Barcelona and taken for a writer most likely going through a depression. The man who wondered about the most beautiful sunrises. She felt as though she would bump into him again someday and return the books.

That young woman, who was to take many such trips in the future, had not yet learned that acquaintances made on long train journeys are never renewed again. Neither, of course, had she ever heard of a famous writer-philosopher named Walter Benjamin who took his own life in the Spanish border town of Portbou.

The Other Twin

Ever since childhood
one side of her face
was condemned to misery.

I didn't write it.
I swear I did not write that letter.
I had no idea it existed.

I knew very little about death or eternity. I associated both with feelings of peril and chaos, like the color black. Although I tried many times, I was never able to conjure an image of eternity; I strove hard to hear it, to feel it and to smell it, but I did not succeed. I still haven't.

Sezin, on the other hand, would draw pictures of eternity even when she was a little girl. Eternity was a window. A window with outstretched wings, ready to take flight. All the windows in her nursery drawings faced eternity. The wide, gaping mouths of crying babies; the eyes of my father who had postponed his joys for another time; the catatonic trances of my mother; the large, industrious hands of Ünzile: these all meant eternity to Sezin. Its color was a shimmering, silvery light. Eternity was that close, that clear and perceivable for Sezin. Within arm's length. As for me, my sense of eternity never developed and never lasted. It never properly existed. It still doesn't.

As a child, I was not striking or special in any way. When regarded separately, all my features were carefully crafted and harmoniously shaded, yet not a single wave played upon my surface that would attract attention. I was like a great lake where all the raging waters lay deep within. I still am.

Sezin, however, was very special. Cheerful, exuberant, and filled with a boundless curiosity for life, she was not only involved in everything but often at the center of it. Her liveliness highlighted her beauty, and, naturally, everyone admired her. I was close enough to her to know that she did not expend any extra energy to attract attention. We were very close, as close as two people can biologically be. Sezin's existence was like that: bright, lively and attractive. It still is.

I never drew attention to myself. No one ever noticed me. I gave the impression of being smaller and weaker than I actually was. I was pastel. I buried excitement and sorrow within myself and lived there all alone. Large, crowded gatherings always frightened me. I felt outside every thing and every person. I felt as distant as could be from every situation. I could only get as far as the borderline; I could never cross it.

I suppose you could call it a sense of redundancy. It seemed as though I disturbed and oppressed others with my presence. I did not have an interesting subject to expound upon or a funny joke to make people laugh, nor did I have the courage to try to look attractive with pretty, come-hither glances. I was pastel.

I hummed songs to myself at such times. Cool, soothing verses that no one could hear. I imagined an overlooked but gorgeous stream. It advanced without betraying any motion; calm, alone and proud. I undressed and swam in that stream as the sun slowly set behind me.

Within myself was where I harbored a hospitable crowd. Where I could throw myself from the highest cliff, where I could exist without fear of causing discomfort or annoyance to anyone. That wilderness, that desolate cliff within me. It still remains the only place.

But I didn't write that letter.
I knew nothing of that letter.

My father. I can't say always, but some of the time . . . I felt close to my father some of the time. The way most children feel close to their mothers. As for my mother, she was always closer to Sezin. My mother is always on the winning side. One year, she became a Galatasaray fan overnight, so enamored was she of the team's victorious season. In order to win, my mother would support whoever had already won. Always. She could not stand being weak, unsuccessful or defeated. That is why she believed Sezin resembled herself, and that is why she had no tolerance for me. She still doesn't.

The kind, flattering words that others offered me never seemed to fit me quite right. I particularly disliked special occasions when such florid praises and exaggerated laughter were bandied about the house. I felt beholden whenever I received gifts or praises; I never believed that I deserved them. Once that feeling of indebtedness takes hold of you it never leaves; like the color of your eyes, it sticks to you all your life and never changes. Until the day you die. Even when you die, the color of your eyes stays the same! The anxious color of indebtedness is a murky, dusty green. My eyes still bear that color.

And finally there was Ünzile. She was the one I was closest to after

Sezin and my dad. Perhaps more than those two, perhaps she was closer to me than both.

Ünzile was always by my side.

She still is.

Ünzile, who entered the household just before Sezin and I were born as fraternal twins, who always remained upstanding and a true family member. Ünzile, the nanny. Dear old Ünzile. Despite her title, she took care of us all. She guarded, she treasured. She devoted herself entirely to us. She still does.

Ünzile was an Anatolian peasant who had never been young, who always looked middle-aged, who was skinny as a pole, stubborn as a mule and strong as an ox. Her face was straight out of a Bruegel painting: sallow skin and androgynous features. Bony, strong hands. Too manly to be a woman and too feminine to be a man. A sexless being. Her posture seemed as though she was always suffering from some ailment that she did not want to disclose. Modest, optimistic, and endowed with the mysterious power to overcome any illness standing up. She explained this as "the strength of the old world and of God." They say that faith, optimism and a natural diet are the most effective nourishment for body and soul. Perhaps she truly was created by Bruegel; who knows.

For years, Ünzile researched the meaning of her own name. When people came for visits she would without so much as a greeting ask them if they knew what Ünzile meant. Upon being denied a satisfactory response, she would declare in a hurt tone that her name was mentioned in the Koran, that it must have had a sacred meaning, and then she would proudly stick her nose in the air. Puzzled and miffed that so many learned ladies and gentlemen did not know the meaning of a simple "Ünzile," she would mumble and potter around the house all night, taking care to make her presence felt.

She still has not found out the meaning of her name, but she has stopped asking everyone who crosses her path. Nowadays she only approaches someone if she likes the look of them, and then brashly instructs them:

"Girls, go get yourselves a good education and figure out for me what this Ünzile means."

Ünzile learned to read and write at the same time we did; she studied math and geography together with us. She became adept at telling time. She was more enthusiastic than we were to piece together puzzles, to fill in coloring books, or to play dress-up with Barbie dolls. She became a fan of Fenerbahçe, Elvis Presley, Kevin Costner, Nilüfer and Sting just like us. But she never did like Mozart.

"This guy, if he had grown up around our parts, who knows what great tunes he would've wrote! What's his name, Mow-zort, or Mo-surht or something? Too bad for the poor infidel."

Although at first her love and aptitude for learning greatly surprised those around her, over the years it became natural to discuss politics, sports and cinema with Ünzile. She always answered Sezin's and my questions patiently and to the best of her ability. What she lacked in knowledge and finesse, she made up for with extraordinary effort, becoming an avid newspaper reader and serious TV viewer in the process. We can never repay her kindness and labor. Especially her patience and effort as she tried to share my ever-deepening silence and Sezin's numerous fields of interest. She was perhaps a true angel.

She still is.

But I knew nothing of that horrible letter.
I did not write that letter.

Ünzile's greatest problem was that she confused my name with

Sezin's. It presented a constant struggle for her. Even when she got our names right, she would second-guess herself, change her mind, and reverse the order. And yet we did not look exactly alike. I was thin and gangly, a brunette with dusty green eyes. Sezin was darker, her eyes were hazel, and she was a little bigger than me. Her nose was prettier. We were fraternal twins.

We still are.

It was not possible for Ünzile to confuse the two of us. It was our names that caused her trouble. With just one letter apart, our names sounded very similar, yet they had different meanings: insight and emotion.

Perhaps it was a game that she had devised in order to put a smile on our lips. After all, her constant befuddlement was an endearing detail. Just a detail. One of hundreds upon which we base our lives . . . That is all.

Sezin was never to blame. I never bore a negative feeling against her. On the contrary, I was very proud to be her twin sister. It was not a fault that her successes, her joy, and most of all her courage made her my exact opposite. I never thought to punish her. Sezin deserved success and attention. She always looked out for me and supported me. But I never liked being the one who was defended and helped.

The venomous victory that gleamed in my mother's eyes when she looked at Sezin was extinguished immediately when she turned her gaze upon me. It broke my heart. She regarded me as a wretch, a piece of dirt that you take care not to get on your clothes. She was absolutely determined never to call me by my name. My twin was called "Sezin," yet I was simply called "girl." Just "girl"! A random, indefinite girl. Her daughter was Sezin. And I was some other girl. Some random girl. My mother avoided getting to know me, dreaded growing close to me. She tried her best not to love me and in the end she succeeded. It was because she did not want to know that she did not love herself. Because confrontation requires courage. Because in fact she is, my mother is . . .

I never knew about that horrible letter.
I don't have any idea who wrote it.
But it wasn't me. I swear upon everyone I love.

My mom and dad never fought. We never saw them argue. But there was an icy, visible wall of silence between them. I did not see them laughing out loud together like my friends' parents, or flinging each other secret, meaningful glances, or cuddling and kissing like in the movies. They never got angry and yelled either. There were no bridges of communication left between them. None!

My mother could only smile with one side of her face. She was such a quiet, contained woman that she could sit in the same room as you for hours without making her presence felt. Her gaze was misty, as if she was always on the verge of tears, and brooding, as though she had sworn to maintain an age-old vow of silence. She complained that everyone on the street stared at her and she preferred to stay hidden away in the house. She read, painted and watched the roofs of other houses from the window. Her paintings did not resemble Sezin's in the least. They frightened me.

When I was a baby they say my grandmother used to call me "scaredy-cat."

My father was a workaholic. He came home late and enjoyed having boisterous conversations about food and politics with Ünzile in the kitchen. If Sezin happened to be awake, he would listen to her breathless retelling of the day's adventures and occasionally interrupt with playful questions designed to puzzle her and throw her off. After pausing and thinking them over briefly, Sezin would come up with cheerful replies and resume her animated narratives. My father and Sezin were a lot alike. They were brave, good-natured, confident and ambitious.

They still are.

My father's only mistake was giving up too soon. But I was the one who was truly to blame! He tried to engage in similar conversations with me; I tried as well. But I lost all my courage when faced with my father's facetious questions and games. He gave up after I ended one too many exchanges by sobbing uncontrollably or lapsing into endless hours of sullen silence. I simply couldn't be brave or confident; I was afraid. I was very easily hurt. Finally he began to treat me like a por-celain doll, like a little girl or even a retarded child. It wasn't his fault. Was it mine? Despite all my efforts, I did not manage to improve our relationship. Worst of all, I never managed to show him my efforts.

I still have not.

I did not write that awful letter.
I swear upon my dearest one's grave.
On Sezin's . . . My father's . . . Ünzile's . . . I didn't write that god-damned letter! I swear on Ünzile's grave . . .

Ünzile was the only person who managed to be close to me. I still shiver to recall the long, cold nights when she wrapped me in a quilt of love and patience, cradling me through endless crying spells, through days of sullen, self-imposed hunger. Besides, wasn't her confusing our names proof that Ünzile, more than anyone, regarded Sezin and me as equals? She loved me as much as the little daughter she had lost long ago, perhaps me in her stead. Perhaps she loved me even more.

She still does.

After my mother was taken to the hospital, the curtains of the house were drawn back, and we started to hear the sound of the radio and the television more often. Sunlight during the day and electricity during the evening helped brush away the dark silence that had formerly pervaded our house. We were told that our mother was ill and required a long treatment before she could recover and return home. No one explained the nature of her illness. We were thirteen at the time.

I dreaded being left alone with my mother. I never set foot in her room, once she had separated it from my father's. She would occasionally summon me inside to view the terrifying paintings she had made, but I never dared to cross the threshold. Nor did I ever enter her room in the hospital. A strange timidity came over me when I approached her room at home, as though she had left one eye behind in the room, ready to spy on me. The human visages in my mother's paintings frightened me to no end. Disproportioned, pained faces, swathes of black that frequently intersected bright surfaces. The color black conjures feelings of danger and chaos within me. Just like eternity.

Sezin and my father went to visit my mother in the hospital several times. I never went. I couldn't bring myself to go. And yet Sezin spoke of our mother with so much hope. Her nerves were a little shaken, she had trouble gathering her thoughts, she had a minor illness inherited from our grandmother, that was all. But her medication was going to cure her in no time. She related these facts as calmly as though they were happening to some other mother and continued her daily life as if nothing had happened. I was in awe of her courage. For my part, I was afraid. Our mother was ill, and if her illness was truly hereditary, we would be next. Us . . . me more than Sezin . . . because I . . .

But I know nothing of that forsaken letter!
I do not have the slightest clue.
I didn't write it!
I swear I know nothing!

My mother returned home after a year. She was even paler and more absent and apathetic than before. She paid absolutely no attention to me or to Ünzile. Her affection for Sezin had increased tenfold; she could not praise her enough. The worst change was in her attitude toward my father. She constantly attacked him, needled him and tried to put him down. I think she was suspicious that he had started seeing another woman during her absence. My mother's suspicions were deadly. She agonized and tortured herself over the most preposterous notions. I could never determine if this agonizing was the cause of her illness or the result of it.

Ünzile did not care much for my mother, yet she seemed resolved not to criticize her. In contrast, my mother did not give a second thought to scolding Ünzile in public. Yet it was my mother who had found her in the village and brought her into our family. Perhaps my mother had been so disappointed with the cowardice and failure of one of her twins that she had fallen ill with grief. And, who knows, perhaps she had consequently lost all affection for both that twin and the woman who loved her.

It wasn't me. It wasn't me who wrote that letter.
I did not have the slightest idea it existed.
Please stop pressuring me, I beg you. Please!

A year after my mother's return, after the hellfire at home had come to be known in the streets and in neighboring homes, my parents got divorced. Ünzile, my father and I moved to another house. My mother stayed in our old house together with Sezin. My mother could not bear to be away from Sezin and could not stand to be around me.

As soon as we had moved into the new house, my father gave me a wonderful gift which I had wanted for years: a little white kitten. My mother did not like animals. They gave her the creeps. Therefore, I had ceased to even fantasize about having a cat of my own. The kitten was everything I could have asked for: a soft, round and warmly affectionate female. Ünzile and I thought long and hard about what name to give her. I was convinced that Little Ünzile was a lovely name for the kitty, but Big Ünzile was scandalized at the idea:

"God forbid, my girl, you might offend the Almighty. We don't know its meaning, but Ünzile is a holy name. Besides, it's a sin to give a human name to a beast!"

That's how we got the notion to baptize my kitten with an animal name. We racked our brains for days, trying to come up with an appropriate animal name for her. My father insisted on Mohini, the name of Turkey's first elephant. Mohini meant "precious one" in Hindi. Ünzile's vote went to Moby Dick, which was the name of a cartoon we used to watch together as I was growing up. We already knew better than to expect such mundane suggestions as Snowball or Mittens from Ünzile. As for me, I was set on the name Kitmir. This was the name of the dog who accompanied the seven magic sleepers.

Ever since we had visited the Cave of the Seven Sleepers in Ephesus during summer vacation, I had felt a particular emotional bond for the dog who, according to the legend, had chosen to fall asleep alongside the people he loved rather than leave them.

My kitten was named Kitmir. That is still her name.

Sezin and I still managed to see each other on a daily basis since we were classmates at school. But her absence was sorely felt in the evenings. Poor Ünzile tried her hardest to make it up for me, running around ceaselessly, trying to make sure I had everything I could possible need. She began to spoil me. That winter she bundled me in colorful hand-knitted clothes, as she somehow reasoned that store-bought clothes might make me feel more motherless. They were warm, soft, love-knitted clothes. She even gave up complaining when I ate a snack before dinner, when I left the refrigerator open, or when I skipped breakfast because I wasn't hungry.

Sezin was still bright and cheerful, still a good student. She did not say much about our mother but she had let it slip that our grandmother's mysterious illness and death years earlier had been suicide. A relative of our late grandmother whom Sezin called "Great Aunt" had moved into our old house.

Still, I knew nothing of that letter!
I swear upon everything I hold dear.
Leave me be. I did NOT write that letter!
I didn't.

I was sixteen when they found the letter. But I only found out about it a year later. It was the summer before my last year of high school. I'd never been an outstanding student like Sezin. As a quiet, unremarkable student, I passed my classes with average grades. My only interest was in psychology. Maybe I had hoped to understand my mother and myself better through studying it. Maybe I'd hoped that it would bring us closer together; I can't say.

My father introduced us to Seçil the first time Kitmir was pregnant. He had invited her over for dinner. By the time I lost count of these invitations, Kitmir had already been neutered, and Seçil had adopted one of her offspring.

Seçil was a colleague of my father's, a redhead who wore glasses. She was eight years younger than my father. She was a cheerful, confident woman who treated us fairly from the start, but who never altered her degree of intimacy. Only my father knew when she was joking. I did not know whether she liked me or not, but I could tell from the first that she was very much in love with my father. And he seemed very happy to be around her.

Seçil won Kitmir over with her particular scent, conquered Ünzile's heart with her cooking skills, and impressed Sezin with her wide range of knowledge and her mastery of three different languages. Her relationship with my father was rife with the camaraderie of old friends, the intimacy of siblings who knew each other's secrets, and the joyful glimmers of a man–woman relationship that were still foreign to me. They loved to trade jokes and complete each other's sentences, and they exchanged mysterious, laughter-filled glances, which I had never seen between my mom and dad.

Seçil was never interested in moving in with us. She always lived in her own house and tactfully implied to us that it was through her own choice.

I tell you I didn't write it. Not me.
I didn't even find out about that letter until months later.
I swear I didn't write it!

They were all panic-stricken when they found the letter. They ran around the house in a flurry of anxious activity. I remember that day, but I had no idea that the mysterious letter and I were the reason for the uproar. Only a year later . . . Only a year later did I discover the existence of such an important document, one that was to affect my life so drastically.

Ünzile never managed to learn Seçil's name. For a while she called her "that redhead of your dad's," then she came up with "Çisil." And since Seçil liked her new moniker, Ünzile came to call her "your dad's Çisil."

"Your dad's Çisil turned out to be a clever one, girls. Goodness, she knows how to please all of us, even Kitmir! Can't say I wasn't wary at first. See, where I come from, redheads are bad luck. That's just what they say . . . Then I was afraid she'd move in and play lady of the house. Well, she's a clever girl alright. But what's the use of all that schooling and diplomas if she doesn't know the meaning of a simple 'Ünzile'?"

Seçil and I had made a silent pact to keep an invisible boundary between us. She approached me from a respectful distance and never made demands or forced her will upon me. It was as though she had sensed the crippling pain of my soul, which I could only reveal to Sezin, Ünzile and Kitmir. She was cool and forthright. She made no bones about the fact that it was our father who she loved and preferred, but it was also clear that we were free to return the sentiment. I was grateful to her for leaving me alone.

No, I didn't write it.
It never crossed my mind, I swear upon my honor.
I was the only one who knew nothing of the letter!

It all started when I agreed to go on vacation with them. Or maybe that's when it all ended. My father had invited me along on the four-day trip that he and Seçil were going to take. Sezin had theater classes and could not get away. At first, I was reluctant. Seçil and my dad needed to spend time alone; they were a new couple after all. But after even Ünzile told me that it would do me good and that I wouldn't bother Çisil in four days, I began to feel hopeful. I decided to go. I packed a small bag with my summer gear. I started anticipating our first easygoing, hysteria-free holiday in years. Nevertheless, I still couldn't muster up any great excitement. If only my mother could have been with us, but if she could be more like Seçil . . . I grew depressed. I don't know what it feels like to experience a joy unclouded by melancholy. I've never felt it.

Early that morning, as we were preparing to leave, the phone rang. Seçil had left her suitcase in the car and had come inside to have breakfast with us. She was busy talking to my father. Ünzile was checking my bag one last time and rattling off a long list of cautionary advice. At first none of us paid attention to my father as he answered the phone, still chewing his breakfast. But the phone would not stop ringing. It rang again as soon as he hung up. When my father's already curt tone rose to a pitch of anger after the fourth or fifth ring, we all began staring at him.

"Please stop crying! You're being ridiculous!" I understood right away that he was talking to my mother. Who knew what had happened this time, or what my mother thought had happened . . .

I ran out of the room in order to say goodbye to Kitmir. When I returned I noticed that all three of them were staring at me strangely. My father, Seçil and Ünzile. All six eyes were fastened on me. Their gaze seemed different somehow.

I had no idea why Ünzile cried piteously as we sped off in the car and she tossed the customary bowl of water behind us for our safe return. Instead of heading south we made a stopover at our old house. As Seçil and I watched from the car, my mother came out of the house sobbing and embraced my father. I attributed her behavior simply to a fit of jealousy and grew embarrassed in front of Seçil. My mother always embarrassed me. My father started the car, unable to conceal his anger, when Sezin came downstairs and gave me a tight hug, telling me to take very, very good care of myself. I had never before seen Sezin so morose.

In the next four days, my father and Seçil paid such close attention to me and treated me so much like a baby that I was sorry I ever went on the trip with them. They did not spend any time alone, they did not have any fun, and they did not even sleep together. Seçil took the single room, claiming that it would be a nice change if I slept in the same room as my father. And my father did not utter a word in protest. I was dying to go back home.

Everyone and everything changed after that trip. Kitmir became skittish around me and began to avoid my company. Ünzile's anxious, pained gaze weighed me down as I tried to do homework, watch TV or just stare at the wall. My father had taken to calling me frequently from work. Seçil had cut back on her visits. Sezin seemed to have lost the exuberance that I so admired in her. At school she took care not to leave my side and stopped paying as much attention to her other friends. Strangest of all, Ünzile had stopped confusing our names. And to top it all off, my mother sent word inviting me over to her house for dinner and a sleepover. My mother!

I was completely baffled. I mulled the situation, turned it over in my head, but could find no explanation. What had happened, what had I done and why wouldn't anyone tell me anything? Or was I becoming a depressed, delusional person like my mother? God protect me! Please, preserve me God,.. I don't want to be like my mother . . . I don't!

All of a sudden, my crying fits grew more frequent, the optimism I'd felt upon moving out of the old house began to wane, and my hopes of growing into a functioning adult started to wither. The feelings of lethargy, pessimism and suspicion within me multiplied like amoebas. I was going through a long painful period in which each feeling intensified grotesquely. Lethargy became a horrible shadow upon a dark curtain, pessimism turned large clouds into many-horned demons, and suspicion seeped out of my armpits as a foul stench. Now no one except Ünzile could approach or touch me. Not Sezin, not Kitmir, not my father . . .

I learned of the existence of the letter purely by accident. I had failed school that year and was repeating my final year while Sezin had started college. One day, Ünzile, who often started crying just looking at me, let it slip by mistake. Without her knowing, without her wanting, it just escaped her lips, Without her wanting at all!

"Oh, my sweet girl, oh, my dear little thing, why do you grieve poor Ünzile so, why do you waste away your youth? Why do you think of death instead of living, loving and enjoying? Why do you write such a crazy letter and drive us half-mad, why . . ."

"A letter?"

"Oh no! What did I say now? Blast my big mouth, what did I say? You stupid old woman, you blabbermouth, you with the accursed name . . ."

A letter? A suicide letter? One that I wrote? Whose death? Sure, I'm lethargic and depressed but I never thought about death. I never even considered my own death. I'm not even eighteen yet . . .

"Ever since we found that letter in your mother's room we've all lost our appetite for life. You burned us right through the heart, my baby girl. It's been over a year now and I still come by your bedside every night and check to hear you breathing; I tremble to think you might take your own life."

So my mother found it? My mother found the suicide letter that I'm supposed to have written but I've never seen or heard of?

"It'll all pass, child. God doesn't leave his followers in a fix; he doesn't keep his messengers for nothing. Who said it was easy to grow up without a mother? I know you've had it hard, child, but you're almost through it, my petal-scented, almond-eyed princess. *Inshallah,* you will find an honest man, and then you can have a brood of your own . . ."

My mother found my suicide letter, written in my handwriting, written in my voice . . .

"See child, you even frightened your mother. See how much she loves you after all, so racked is she with grief. And why would you ever think that you were a burden to us? How could you possibly get that in your head, my pretty little dove?"

And I'm supposed to have written this letter? I'm telling you, I've never heard of this letter, I know nothing about it!

"For some reason your dad's Çisil won't believe that you wrote that letter. She's never believed it. She just keeps on saying 'Sezin couldn't have written that letter!' but your dad saw your handwriting with his own eyes."

I never even entered my mother's room . . . The few times Ünzile had badgered me into accepting my mother's invitations, I had taken care to avoid even the bathroom of our old house. I swear I didn't write it, I didn't even know it existed! But they—except for Seçil—they had all believed that I had written a suicide note. Easily, quickly, just like that. Maybe because they had expected something like this from me all along, they were convinced of it in a second. Maybe they expected . . .

For months I sought the author of that letter. I chased the person who had forged a suicide note in my name and placed it in my mother's room. Sezin changed the subject whenever I brought it up. The events of the past did not concern her. Ünzile's heart, which had aged in the past two years, could not withstand any discussion of the subject lest she fall ill. My father acted as though nothing had happened, so steadfast was he in his belief that time healed all wounds. I was too timid to talk to Seçil. As for my mother, she had started drinking heavily. Her teeth had turned nicotine-yellow, and dark, heavy bags hung beneath her eyes. Her mouth and neck had become crisscrossed with wrinkles. She seemed to have collapsed entirely in the last two or three years. I was afraid of my mother. I was afraid of her person, her paintings, and of growing up to resemble her . . .

That year, after graduating from secondary school, I earned a place in the Psychology department at the university. You could say that I was a little excited and hopeful. But university life did not bring about any of the changes I had hoped for. I was still shy, dull and lonely. I was pastel. I fled from people who approached me and then regretted it for days. I imagined that they were after my scrupulous lecture notes and my language skills rather than my friendship. But my true obsession was trying to find the person who had forged that letter and left it in my mother's house. It had become my only goal, my only reason for living! My only ambitious pursuit in the world! That letter!

My search proved fruitless. That year and the next. I knew that the person who tried to eliminate herself by killing me was lurking nearby, and I still failed to find her. Feeling her breath on my neck . . . She who had branded me with the icy touch of death . . . She who shuddered with horror at my mirror image every time she laid eyes on me . . . She who had always kept me apart from my twin . . .

I could not find her. Knowing . . . searching . . . burning . . .

Then I wrote it.

I wrote it.

This time, it really was me.

I wrote the letter expected of me.

Three years after the fake letter, I produced a real version:

I am finally leaving.
It is not anybody's fault.
I really am writing the letter this time.
This time I'm leaving for good.
Sezen (The Other Twin)

Ünzile found her.

She sank to her knees and began to wail and beat herself. Seçil tried to tend the father, who was still begging the doctors for a glimmer of hope, but she kept collapsing in tears on the sofa. The house was filled with relatives and neighbors and the pervasive scent of lemon cologne. The mother, who was muttering unintelligible phrases to herself while chain-smoking madly, screamed at the guests to throw out the white cat who was meowing pitifully at the head of the corpse. The atmosphere was thick with cologne, spent life, and sorrow.

A week later, Ünzile packed her bags and her memories and, despite all protests, prepared to return to her village. As he was seeing her off, the father asked:

"You were her closest to her, Ünzile. Maybe you would know: Why did Sezen sign that letter 'The Other Twin'? Although it's too late, I want to have a glimpse into my daughter's closed world. You understand, don't you?"

Racked with pain, Ünzile narrowed her eyes, which were chafed from crying:

"Sir, it was a game my girl Sezen played! It was a joke between us. My little dove had figured a twin for herself and called her Sezin. That's who she lived with most of the time. Sometimes, to confuse me, she'd switch from Sezin to Sezen. It was a special secret we kept between us from the time she was a little girl. What does it matter now if you know or not? The other twin was just a game, a soul mate that my precious, unfortunate girl had invented for herself."

The Soul That Loves Not Istanbul, What Does It Know of Love?*

"Foreigners call *Haliç* 'the Golden Horn.' Istanbul is the only city in the world with a golden horn." So she said. Not one word less, not one word more. And she said it often. Then her dreamy eyes wandered far, far away. I could never tell if she was yearning for the sweethearts of her Istanbul girlhood or if she was regretting other missed chances. In either case, I was too young to know that love, whether lived or imagined, grows hazy behind the veil of time.

"The only city in the world with a golden horn!"

Every time I heard her utter these words a door flew open before me to reveal the large and swarthy figure of a bull. I could not have known then why the word "horn" reminded me of a bull and not a stag or an ox. But each time I heard or imagined the phrase "city of the Golden Horn," this enormous, angry bull charged towards me. And with such ferocity! It galloped forth, hellbent on my destruction, my obliteration! It startled me. Worse, it frightened me. My knees grew weak and I started to tremble. I was terrified. Yet despite my terror, I always noticed the youth and beauty of the bull. Then I shut

---

* This title is a verse from the poem "Kalamış" by Behçet Kemal Çağlar.

my eyes and braced myself for the impact. Fear rooted me to the spot every time. And yet I was enthralled by the bull's sense of strength and vitality, by the health and abundance it exuded. My awe mingled with my rising terror to create a feeling of inferiority. When combined, these two strong emotions cause a kind of voluntary submission: the peril of addiction and the languor of hypnosis.

The bull never attacked. Through some kind of miracle, he always stopped short of charging me. When I reopened my eyes to find myself face to face with the bull, we looked at each other in utter surprise. For we both noticed that he had a handicap, a handicap that, through divine grace, had been transformed into an incredible beauty. The bull lacked a horn. In the middle of his forehead, the bull sported a single horn that gleamed brightly as it curved toward the sky. He was the one and only golden-horned bull! He was a legend! He was truly a legend! When I managed to tear my eyes away from the golden horn that reached toward Istanbul's high vistas, I met his sad and sorrowful eyes. His soft brown eyes, in direct contrast to his strong, large and virile body, pored over me tenderly. That was when I first experienced the aesthetic harmony of opposites, although it ran contrary to conventional wisdom. I was bathed in a strange light and felt an unfamiliar joy course through my body.

Having recovered from my terror, I gazed at the brilliant golden horn in admiration, while he, knowing he was different from all other bulls, stood with sorrow but also with the strength of acceptance. That most painful and lonely moment of acceptance. It was because of that mythical bull that I learned the difficulty and pain of acceptance. I witnessed that moment with my own eyes. How many people can say that they have personally beheld a moment of acceptance? We labor so painstakingly to conceal from ourselves our own such moments . . . Well, I always knew he was a different bull. He was special, lonely and luminous. He was born as a symbol of power, abundance, rage and aggression, but his mythic handicap lent his eyes an affectionate sorrow. He was Istanbul: the Bull of Istanbul. It was also around this time that I first encountered the agony of conflicting feelings: admiration and pity. Pity smells like vinegar; admiration like vanilla. To this day, I have always disliked vinegar and bullfights. As for vanilla, anything and everything that contains vanilla immediately seduces and captivates me.

"The only city with a sea running through it," she would say. Her eyes dreamy, her voice filled with poetry, she would become lost in thought. Istanbul was the only city in the world that had a sea running through it. My god, what must that be like? How would I feel if a sea ran through me?

It made me think of Deniz. Deniz, riding his bike, playing football, singing songs. Deniz, who thrilled me with his utter lack of self-consciousness. Deniz, beautifully absorbed in his every occupation. I was as yet unfamiliar with the artificiality of those who are terminally self-conscious, or the sincerity of those who become completely absorbed in their occupations. I was also too inexperienced to know that emotional poverty is a product of arrogance and artificiality, and that the pleasure of lovemaking lies in its heated intimacy and frankness. Or you could say that I had a long walk ahead of me before I could discover my own pleasures and truths. All I knew was that Deniz was my best friend and I loved to play with him, as he loved to play with me. So much.

I was so curious to know the feeling of being traversed by a sea that I immediately thought of Deniz, who was named after this body of water. Deniz was an active and fickle child. He was volatile and irrepressible. Because he hated barbers, his fine brown hair grew down to his shoulders in the summer. Neither his mom nor his dad could ever succeed in dragging him to the barber. And so I imagined Deniz as a mercurial being, made up entirely of his hair. I imagined him easily and very often. I dreamed of him incessantly. Deniz, made up of his long, fine hair, entered through my mouth and flowed through me. "Hooray, Deniz is passing through me, now I am Istanbul!" I would then think. I would feel a tickle in my throat and a funny sensation in my stomach, but I still liked it. But Deniz did not behave. If the urge took him, he dispersed through my entire body, travelled up to my tear ducts and itched me there. He made me cry inexplicably. When Deniz swerved toward my ears, I felt dizzy and my ears rang. If he spent too long in my inner ear I became dizzy and queasy. Deniz trickled down to my armpits. He tickled me. I would laugh and snort suddenly. Deniz knew that I was easily tickled. Deniz knew me well. Just as I became delirious with laughter Deniz headed toward my nose. I felt an itch, then I would sneeze, Achoo! Bless you! We were young, Deniz and I, we were young enough to believe all my dreams, but still I would feel a giddiness, a faintness as he passed through my loins, still, I would . . .

That's when I knew. I knew why in the only city in the world bisected by a sea anything could happen at any moment. Istanbul could suddenly rear its head and roar; it might sneeze and disperse sensuous pleasures all through your body. Istanbul possessed a rage powerful enough to crush and obliterate you. Istanbul had the breadth of imagination and depth of heart to inebriate you with feeling, to sweep you off your feet with joy. For the sea ran through Istanbul.

Deniz was not like anyone else. Behind his calm and sweet exterior, Deniz was hyperactive, difficult and stubborn. Then again, how could a city cut by the sea remain temperate and unperturbed; how could it stay reticent and calm? Deniz was unpredictable, unknowable, and therein lay the root of his beauty. I loved to play with him, as he loved to play with me. So much.

Interestingly enough, I did not live at the time in that city of the Golden Horn, the city bisected by the sea. It was my mother who related to me, with dreamy eyes and lingering voice, the city of her girlhood years. After marrying my father, who was a native of Ankara, she had settled down to raise me in his hometown. Yet her dreams and her spirit had remained in Istanbul. My father had grown up proud to be a native Ankaran and he bravely defended his Ankara, which was not divided by a sea and which did not possess a golden horn, against my mother's Istanbul during their frequently fought "Battle of the Cities." "If it hadn't been for Ankara, you would have to get a passport to visit your precious Istanbul," he said. My father's voice was devoid of languor or hushed respect. His voice was deep, dependable and decisive. No sea had wound its way through his heart. I understood. Ankara and Istanbul had different voices, but both were as close and necessary to me as my mother and father. I understood. Istanbul's one half was in Asia and its other half in Europe. My mother's and father's voices were different. I understood.

"But you always wanted to leave, to visit distant lands," he said.

I had finally learned the difference between real and imagined love, between the aftertastes of love and separation. I had learned where anger and pain could stab you. I had grown up. I had suffered and bled at the hands of disappointment and betrayal; I had disappointed and inadvertently hurt others, but I had never betrayed them. So far, I had matured, I still had an aversion to vinegar and bullfights, I still loved anything that contained vanilla, and I frequently thought about my childhood with Deniz.

"Yes, that's true," I replied. "When you're young, you sincerely believe that you can find perfection, the unsurpassable, or at least the harmonious. You look for something different, for the *other*. You search far and wide, following tracks, signs and scents. Many were the years when I thought 'there is such a thing as perfection, it must exist somewhere.' I swear to you, I thought it possible." My voice was not cold or bitter. My voice was mature.

"You were always the one who took off, who had to keep seeking, who couldn't be satisfied. You sent yourself into exile. And now you're back in Istanbul and you come to me as if none of this ever happened, as if you'd never left, never taken anything with you when you left. You're being unfair. You are unfair."

"Istanbul was too Eastern then, and I was too much of a Westerner. Istanbul was too hectic, messy, aggressive, wrathful and old. What seemed exotic to me at the time was the orderly, the clean, the calm and the new. Istanbul was dark-complexioned, and naturally, for me, exotic was blond. I fled from Istanbul. I was afraid of its destructive power, my knees trembled under its might. I shunned *rakı* for wine, I looked down on our tulip-shaped teacups and instead used mugs; I was too good for *simit* so I ate bagels, croissants and pastries. I was only nineteen," I said.

"We were nineteen," he corrected me.

"Nineteen," I echoed.

"Did you have to go?" he asked.

His voice was not angry or accusing. Neither did it betray resentment or vengefulness. His voice conveyed a desire to understand. Hearing this desire made me feel hopeful.

"I had to leave so that I could return and understand. Some of us need to leave," I said.

He sighed.

So did I.

Every summer, without fail, my mother would take my family to

Istanbul. During our stays, she would exhaust herself trying to show us her city. She labored ceaselessly, like a tour guide who risked losing house and home it she failed to enamor us of the city. It was as though the world might come to a standstill if we did not see, perceive and love her Istanbul. Why, I wonder, did my mother strive so hard?

She wore elegant, pale dresses with tapered sleeves, which she had sewed herself, She put on white-framed sunglasses with upturned edges. She wore white, domestic brand Capri slides. Neither her shoes nor her clothes were expensive but they always looked stylish and prim on her. I remember my mother best in these outfits, smiling delightedly on the citywide ferry, sipping tea from a tulip-shaped glass.

"They've diluted this tea with baking soda, it tastes awful but I always buy one just for tradition's sake," she'd say. She told us of the Maiden Tower every time we took the ferry. She forgot her surroundings and, imagining that we were alone, raised her voice to tell us of the Maiden Tower.

My father listened along with the other passengers on deck, taking care to maintain his composure, ignore the diluted tea and conceal his pride in her. (I knew that my father was proud of my mother, but she didn't. Women do not know without hearing; children understand.) My father was there, beside us; my father was with us, but my mother was divided by the sea. This was the reason why she was happy in Istanbul. There was nothing that pleased my mother more than Istanbul; not the religious festivals featuring Ankara's mouthwatering roll-up pastries; not the family dinners for which Grandma cooked her famous Ankara stew; not our frequent visits to Atatürk's mausoleum, which were propelled by her devout nationalism; not our visits to the zoo, where we saw Mohini the Indian elephant . . . If there was anything that pleased her as much as Istanbul, I did not know of it.

"The Maiden Tower," she would intone, with dreamy eyes and breathless voice. "It is one of the oldest lighthouses with a known history. It is said to have been built before the prophet Jesus. This isn't any old lighthouse. The Maiden Tower is beautiful because of its legend."

She told us the story of the Maiden Tower as we passed by it on our obligatory ferry trip during our annual summer pilgrimage to Istanbul. Upon learning that his daughter's fate is to die of a poisonous snakebite, the king cloisters the lovely princess (why they're always lovely is beyond me) in the Maiden Tower for many long years. But can anyone escape their fate? (Of course they can, Mom!) Years later, a snake concealed in a basket of grapes manages to penetrate the tower and administer the fated, fatal bite to the lovely and lonely princess. So the snake kills the princess (that's why I confused her with Cleopatra). As for the grapes, they take their place in Istanbul's history.

On some trips, the princess was the daughter of an Ottoman emperor, and on others she came from a Byzantine lineage. None of us minded. Her ethnic and religious identity did not concern us in the least, but we all mourned her cruel fate. If the legend of the Maiden Tower changed slightly every year, if an oil lamp or a torch lit the chamber instead of a light bulb, if the stories were Athenian, Spartan, Greek, Byzantine, Arabian, Ottoman or Turkish, none of it made a difference. This tower had a legend. The truth is that legends are not easy to come by, and not every place or person can boast of one.

"Then one day you return, despite all those worn, estranged and perhaps even diminished feelings," he said.

"Yes."

My voice is clear. Distilled through years of experience, it has lived and loved, fought and conquered; it has become my own. Both Deniz and I have quit smoking and turned forty.

"Yes, all my flights, all the new people, new cities, countries, continents, new loves, separations, disappointments, pains, discoveries . . . they all happened so I could return."

"Sounds just like you," he said.

Good god, how lovely it is to talk to your soul mate! I know how much or how little he understands me, I trust the sincerity of all his shortcomings, I am certain that his post-lovemaking peck is no personal insult; he is my soul mate! Istanbul, my soul mate.

"You are the queen of contradictions! You always have been. You made me fall in love with Istanbul with all your holiday tales, your half-baked legends, and then you left," he grumbled.

Grumbling implies emotion. Emotion is hope. I grew elated thinking "He loves me, he still loves me!"

"I used to live in a small town in Western Europe."

He stared at me to see if I was joking.

"How preposterous!" I laughed.

He laughed as well. I had missed his laugh, the one that had irritated me for so many years. I missed it because it was genuine. When he was very hurt he retaliated with this laugh. He irritated me no end.

"One night I was walking around in that small European town— and by no means do I belittle it by calling it small, for despite its population of two hundred and fifty thousand, it had two art museums, fifteen public libraries and one serious university—anyhow, one night I was walking around town with a friend."

His face darkened. Obviously, he thought I was talking about a European lover. I was glad to be able to read his thoughts. If you can perceive that the other person has misperceived, you may still have a chance of communicating.

"A *girl* friend," I added.

Our eyes met. He understood that I understood. He was pleased to understand that I understood. We had met enough people, suffered enough pain and felt enough despair to know the rarity of such instances. We had experienced it together and on our own. He smiled. He was glad to recognize me.

"That night we stood on a bridge in the little town, the girl turned to me and asked: 'Isn't it beautiful?' I looked out. It was truly beautiful. There was something in it that seemed exotic to us. It was a tidy, clean city with grid-like streets and orderly, twinkling lights. It was beautiful. And very boring. I felt this clearly for the first time when I was with that girl. The town was meticulously planned and comfortable. It was never subjected to blackouts; the fire department and paramedics were reliable institutions. The police were forbidden to torture their own people, the mayor and local politicians were approachable, accountable people who were not above the law. No one was concerned with what women wore or who they slept with. There were no filthy rich people with questionable sources of wealth or dirt-poor folk without any hope for the future. This is where the real excitement lay. Not the city itself. The city did not even have a personality."

I paused for a breath. He was listening to me intently.

"The small town European girl turned to me on that bridge and, gesturing with one arm toward the city, declared 'This is my town!' Her voice was incredibly proud, drunk with a sense of ownership, and her eyes sparkled. She was ecstatic. I'll never forget that moment. I envied her, do you know that? I envied the naive love, dedication and belonging she felt for a city that never did nor ever would have a history, a legend, a tale or a miracle."

"Yet you struggled for years against belonging to any one person or place," he remarked, his voice woeful.

"I fought for years to free myself of all my cultural, economic and political chains, to be free of owning or being owned. I refused. God, how hard it is to refuse sometimes. Especially during times of hardship, refusal requires willpower. And each refusal expands the boundaries of one's loneliness. You know how it goes," I said, running out of breath. "I did not belong to my town. I had no regular city or country address, no regular job, no steady lover, husband, child or family. I was infinitely independent and unfettered. I was hungry but free."

"You went into exile," he said. "You wanted to find out what it was like to be left alone, devoid of any ties or roots. You wanted to see how far you could push all your boundaries. Just like when we were kids. You always strained the boundaries of our fantasies, our pretend games. You used to drive me crazy, You tore apart my boundaries."

He was right. Only then did I understand he was right. Only then could he express his rightness:

"You were unchained and unrestrained but you were afraid of losing your way. So you wrote like mad. You wrote an incredible amount. I could not keep up with your letters. Your stories, diaries, essays and poems. You were reverting to your mother tongue in order to keep from getting lost. Writing had become your compass, your clock, your calendar."

It was true. I was a product of my mother, who was more in love with Istanbul's legends than the city itself, and my father, who fervently believed in Ankara's homely veracity; I was the person they raised in the light of dreams and realities. In the end, this opposition had turned in to a mass of contradictions. He was right; I loved him, but I'd been too scared to stay with him. For there was something I'd wanted more than him: I'd wanted to become lost and found again, to be reborn and recreate myself; I'd wanted to create my own legend, to live.

"Perhaps you were afraid of getting lost," he said. "You ran back to me every time. As for me, I had fallen in love with the Istanbul you always told me about, I had followed you there after high school and made it my home. I hated you every time you left, but like the one-horned bull, you were very special, very attractive and addictive. You were indispensable. Each time you returned, I, and this city, welcomed you with open arms, and I hated myself for it; the conflict of love and hate tore me apart."

"Like Istanbul," I thought.

"It was as though I sat and waited here just for you, without doing anything else, praying that you'd return alone and virgin, like the Maiden Tower itself."

He completed medical school. Unlike me, he was a good student. He specialized in psychiatry. "Woman, I became a doctor of myths in order to understand you better," he would say, laughing. He married and divorced twice. He had one daughter, now a teenager. Her name: Efsâne, "Legend."

"Watching that small, boring and meticulous western European town, I knew that I'd never be able to run away from Istanbul. Or from you. This realization frightened me even more, so in the next few years I changed my address and my lifestyle even more frequently."

He stared at me to see if I was joking.

"Even those of us who hate it have a few melodramas within us. There is a drama queen in all of us, waiting to emerge," I said mockingly.

We fell silent. I knew he was weighing my words as a doctor. As a person, he already agreed with me wholeheartedly. A person only learns to recognize their beloved's truths after their own have been recognized. I was his melodrama.

"Years later, that small town girl came to visit Istanbul. It hit her hard. It made a mess of her. She was struck as much by the legends, the history, the culture and the beauty of Istanbul as the barbarism, the disorder, the poverty and energy of it. She suffered the plight of a model student who is left to face a question much larger than the ones she has learned and prepared for. Though at first she tried to smile, she finally began to moan. She was not used to these questions; she wanted the questions to which she knew the answers. She wanted to enjoy the feeling of being the best in her class, to get good grades once again. Istanbul was mysterious, unstable, difficult and extremely beautiful. She turned and ran back home. 'How do you people live here?' she said on her way to the airport. Now she visits every summer—and owns a house on Heybeli Island."

I looked at him. He was concentrating on a pattern in the carpet. He was weighing my words. He did not want a new melodrama but he could not give it up. His hair was still playful as in his boyhood, but now it was short. Now he went to the barber himself. He had patches of gray and had gained some weight. Still, he had not let himself go. I gazed at him intensely, with all my being. Sensing that he was still capable of mischief, I grew happy. Though it was well concealed from the outside, inside he still had not turned into a calm, obedient and complacent person. I understood. My soul mate, my dearest friend, my love full of contradictions.

"Deniz," I said, trembling. "Come, Deniz, and flow through me."

That's when Deniz reared his head and looked at me. He looked at me like he used to when as a child I told him of Istanbul's legends. He gazed at me, begging to believe but showing that he did not. Deniz looked at me.

"Istanbul is still an Easterner, it's still old and angry. In fact, it's more aggressive than before and it smells of rakı. Istanbul hasn't changed much," he said wearily.

"But I have, I am just as much an Easterner as Istanbul. I am as old as Istanbul, I am as Mediterranean, as Balkan, as European as Istanbul. I want rakı and wine, I want order and chaos, I want love and rage."

"You'll leave again," he said.

It was as though he was ready to believe me if I said no, as though a tiny "no" could convince him instantly.

"I'm a compass, Deniz. I've become a drawing compass now."

"You were that raging bull as a child. With your sorrow and your anger, with your might and your loneliness . . ."

"Now I'm a compass," I said.

He looked at me quizzically, wondering if this was another legend, and waited.

"My sharp end is anchored in Istanbul, my drawing leg spins around it . . ."

He laughed. "Like the dervishes," he said.

His heart had come running back to me together with his voice, but his body was still far away. It was not only me he was uncertain of, it was also himself. I was not the sole reason for my departures. I had not parted from him all those times just for the sake of leaving. Deniz finally knew. Deniz was never an easy person. Deniz could not be a calm, silent, manageable person. Does any sea resemble still waters? Now he knew himself well enough that he could not blame me entirely.

"You've understood love, O bull of the golden horn, O raging and compassionate bull," he said to me.

"And you, Deniz?" I asked.

He did not reply.

We were silent for a while.

"We'll not know unless we try, once again, with thrill and terror, once again . . ." he said.

He was holding back but that was his way. In the end, I was the one lacking a horn, but that single golden horn gave me my legend. He knew this.

"Come, flow through me, Deniz."

Deniz looked at me.

Deniz approached me.

Mary Magdalene Won't Be Ashamed Anymore

Everybody has a travel story. Some are short, some are long, some are funny, some are entrancing. Some leave their trace as they strike you and go, some are straight and colorless, and some are mysterious, even dangerous. Some challenge, some certainly tempt you to embark on a journey of your own. There is always a travel story; everybody has one. And each person's travel story is the most important one.

My travel story is not that interesting. You know, one day one gets bored even with oneself. Actually, one gets the most bored with oneself. I've been on the road for years. Once things that are interesting and exotic when initially discovered start to become routine and ordinary, the traveler's greatest fear appears. Suspended above the traveler's restless soul that is burning to flee is a very sharp sword that can drop at any moment: the fear of routine; in other words, a settlement phobia. Every restless soul knows that this sword means death, and so traveling is another name for the flight from death.

Trains, ferries, cabs, subways, trucks to be hitchhiked, train stations, wharves, backpacks, suitcases, tents, hostels, dormitories, banks at stations, homes of friends, sofas, sleeping bags . . . Address books, post offices, postcards, email addresses, internet cafés, pocket guides and maps . . . At each stop, short-term, menial jobs, earning money just to survive . . . Then the same things, over and over again . . . Whatever you do, the danger is that it will start repeating itself. And the slow but anxious realization that every city or town traveled, every valley or forest seen, every experience lived is similar . . . Dusks filled with sorrow that human stories are so similar . . . Sudden panic . . . The emotional state in which you feel overwhelmed, do not enjoy anything, and that anxiety . . . It was on just one of those days that I woke up in the morning with a brilliant idea. I found a solution so that I would never relive anything again and would never be bored. I would make traveling my work: I was going to search for the best travel stories and collect those I liked the most. Yes, just like that, I was going to buy travel stories, compile and sell them, and thereby the mysteries and beauties, sins and shames of other people's lives would be in my hands, and after that benevolent angel called Time had passed, I would hand them over to others. As Goethe said, "Sin and shame cannot be kept secret," or shouldn't be.

I started right away, and, as you see, I'm still doing this job without getting bored at all. I don't know if I need to tell you, but just as in any profession, expertise is important in mine too. In the job of collecting travel stories, it is vital to recognize fake, copied or pirated products immediately.

As you've understood by now, my office is the road, and my working medium the train, because only on train trips can one find the time, place and peace to collect travel stories. The purpose for my presence before you right now is to tell you a fine travel story that I've bought, because I'm sure there is one among you who is bored, finds their life unbearable, or wishes they were somewhere else, in someone else's shoes, or would simply like to listen to a good travel story. I will tell this story to that person, and almost for free.

I think it was about ten years ago. I was traveling on a train from the dark Northern European winter to the Mediterranean that is a great gift of God to humankind. While walking up and down the train searching for the person from whom to buy the best travel story, I ran into her every time I crossed the corridor, but I wanted to see all of the passengers before I made my final decision. She was a young woman. She was listening to a Walkman, making notes in a travel notebook, and nibbling on a green apple. When I saw that she had a fresh apple in her hand each time I passed her, I became curious. Her backpack must have been full of green apples. This is how I understood the first sign: she didn't have money for food and instead stuffed her stomach with apples; an experienced traveler learns the practical advantages of eating apples on journeys. And when I saw that she was holding these three travel books, I decided she was the passenger I was looking for: Jack Kerouac's *On the Road*, Steinbeck's *Travels with Charley*, and Reşat Nuri Güntekin's *Notes from Anatolia*.

It is easy to befriend people on train trips because train trip friendships are temporary. I approached and greeted her. She greeted me back.

"Granny Smiths are delicious," I said.

"How sad that they brand green apples," she sneered, and continued, "Would it be more reasonable to go directly to Malaga or to get off in Barcelona?"

She had understood I was a traveler myself.

"If you like Picasso, first Malaga," I said.

Then, pointing at the apple in her hand, I said, "I can buy you an exquisite lunch if you sell me something in return."

Her eyebrows rose, and with an amazed look on her face, she searched my face carefully. I was most serious and sincere.

"Interesting . . . What do you buy?"

"The best travel stories," I said.

She burst into laughter. She cheered up. I laughed too. I was by then a middle-aged traveler and had learned that different kinds of laughter had different meanings. The young traveler woman had believed me.

"What are you going to do with the travel story of someone you don't know at all?" she asked, still smiling.

"That's my job. I buy the travel stories of travelers I don't know at all."

"Always buying them a meal?"

"Sometimes a place to sleep, sometimes paying for the ticket for their next journey, and sometimes buying them a book, bag or drink they desire," I said.

She considered this for a while. Then she looked at me again.

"You have a nice job. You're very lucky," she said.

I was waiting patiently.

"But no private questions and no contact afterwards," she warned me.

"Definitely not. I'm just going to listen."

"Okay!" she said.

As we were talking in a third language that wasn't native for either of us, I couldn't figure out whether she said that thinking of "OK" or "Okay."

After an hour, while I was waiting for her to finish the meal she was eating with gusto at a small table covered with a white linen table cloth in the dining car, I was expecting that the travel story she was about to tell would be of an Eastern Mediterranean clime, but I was wrong; her story came from the North. As we were sipping our coffee accompanied by chocolate cake, she began to tell the story.

"Our story takes place in a distant land. We are in a faraway country whose lakes cannot be counted exactly. All of the lakes remain frozen for months. Despite that fact, this person always rides a bike. Riding a bike on ice is very difficult, especially when you know that there is deep water under the ice," she said.

"I had spent the summer in the Sahara Desert and then had gone to the North, where the winters pass in a gothic darkness. That wasn't a conscious decision. It just happened to be that way . . . You know, your direction on your travel map can change due to love, a special project, or curiosity. At that time my reason was love. Yes, love. A very blue-eyed, baby-faced love with lots of sugar. Love is beautiful."

She fell silent and looked at the picture of her love in her coffee cup. I thought that she still loved that blue-eyed, baby-faced man.

"I was broke. I didn't have a residence or work permit. I was lonely. I was down. You know, one of those hard times that you frequently go through while you are traveling . . ."

She took another sip of her coffee, which I thought must have become cold by then. I understood that she was a real coffee fan from the way she held the coffee cup in both of her hands, compassionately. I was going to buy her another cup of coffee if I liked her story.

"My boyfriend had left me. Though I couldn't accept it at the time, that was the fact. It hurts to be left. The reason never matters; it is painful to be left. Always. But anyway, I was left. It was one of those times when I felt I had no place to go back to. You know, those wars of pride when you cannot accept defeat but are in fact defeated. The mood of angrily searching for other ways out . . . but there was no branch left to hold onto so as not to fall. It was winter, it was dark, it was the far North. I was penniless, I was in a miserable situation. You know . . . All the factors were leading to depression; it was waiting for me. My morale was destroyed, I thought that everybody except me was lucky. Worst of all, I had started to feel pity for myself. I was sleeping in a sleeping bag in the kitchen of two of my girlfriends for the time. Then one day I saw an ad for a book in a newspaper. It was in this ad for a poetry book that I saw the name Mary Magdalene, in a language I didn't know, in a newspaper of which I didn't understand even a single line. Next to the book, which I understood was a poetry book because of the arrangement of the lines, was a picture of the poet. The poet was a woman. Women poets always make me sad. They are the ones, I think, that are the loneliest among creative artists. I found out that the title of the book meant 'Mary Magdalene won't cry anymore.' You know, the prostitute that Jesus saved from a sinful life—the woman that was always ashamed of her name even though she later became a saint. Of course I didn't know this story back then."

Suddenly she stopped and remembered:

"But you are coming from a Christian culture, you already know Mary Magdalene. Why explain it to you? Actually, are you coming from a Christian culture? " she asked.

I waited without saying anything. I didn't know whether she was looking for Jewish traces on my face, but she gave up anyway.

"The book consisted of rebellious poems about Mary Magdalene, saying that this woman who had tortured herself for centuries for being a prostitute should not feel ashamed anymore. The name of the poet was Fairy Tale. Look, I'm not kidding. The woman's name really was Fairy Tale. That is, the name of the poet was a word in the language of that country that meant 'fairy tale.' I found the telephone number of the poet called Fairy Tale from the directory, and called her. I told her that I was a foreign traveler living in the same city as her, and that I liked the rebellion and feminine poeticism in a verse that was translated for me. She listened to me and immediately invited me to her house. That evening, I had dinner with the woman poet called Fairy Tale at her place."

The travel story had started well. I hadn't figured out yet what portion of what she told was true, but I was going to understand that at the end anyway. She, on the other hand, had forgotten me while telling her best travel story. That was a good sign.

"Fairy Tale was very tall and had fair skin and black hair. People born in the Karelia region of that Northern country had black hair, contrary to all Northern laws. Like the Laz jokes in my country about people from the Black Sea region, in her country, there were Karelia jokes. In other words, Fairy Tale was coming from an origin that had irony and a strong tradition of humor. In a wooden house on a lake, she was living with her two daughters and several cats. She had a simple and plain lifestyle, which is the most beautiful characteristic of Northern culture. At the table in the kitchen we had simple and healthy vegetable dishes and wine. You know, alcohol is very precious in Northern countries; there, you can only buy it from the state-owned liquor stores, and of course that's only if you have enough money to buy it, given the very high taxes. Fairy Tale was distant, quiet, controlled, but helpful and brave at the same time. She was an interesting and nice woman. That evening, I learned that she had an engineering degree, that she was working as a researcher in the city's technical university, and that she had been divorced recently. She, in turn, learned similar things about me."

I was beginning to get a little bored. The travel story that had started quite well had lost pace. I wasn't going to insist on buying her the second coffee.

"Within a month, with the help of her reference, I had found a short-term but good research job at the technical university where Fairy Tale worked. I was working on an environmental project with scientists from all over the world. It was around the time when the Green movement first started to make its voice heard in the world. I rented a small pension room for myself, started to eat properly, and made friends. However, you also know that travelers' stories don't last long. Long stories require settling and being part of the system. So, naturally, it didn't last long. Towards the end of the year, I was in trouble with the police, at risk of being unable to extend my work permit. I couldn't get my wages although I was working; I was broke once again. I lived on potatoes and had difficulty paying the rent for my room. Fairy Tale's situation wasn't too bright either. She was writing her first novel, she had to think about the expenses of her growing daughters and about her master's thesis. I can't say we were joyful. No, we weren't. The days we were living were not so wonderful, but don't misunderstand me, we still were not unhappy. It was white all over, very cold and dark. Still, we had become close friends. We had long and profound conversations at the kitchen table in her house overlooking the lake, and we would take walks along the lakeshore. The most beautiful memories of our lives are the traces of the most intense emotional moments that we share with the people we feel closest to. That's how it was . . . However, those walks by the lake were real torture for me. Remember, I'm a Mediterranean; I'm always so cold that it makes Northern people laugh. Yes, we were broke, but not unhappy. We had plans and hopes for the future. We were going to write books, raise children, have love affairs, travel around the world, leave our traces in the world, and definitely succeed."

Her face was brightened by an impish smile. I had understood that she was one of those smart people who don't wait for all external conditions to be perfect in order to be happy. I like smart people. But I was surprised that I hadn't been able to figure out that she was a scientist. I also like those people who still can surprise me at this age.

"I'm not that pious, but I like to celebrate feasts of all religions and cultures. Celebration and entertainment are the greatest inventions of humankind. On Christmas Eve, we were ready for a gloomy little celebration in Fairy Tale's house overlooking the lake, together with her daughters, cats, various potato dishes and a small bottle of spirits. Our table was almost empty. We had lit candles and decorated the plastic pine tree with the colored covers of tea bags. That the tree was made of plastic was very significant to Fairy Tale. Even at that time, she was a registered member of many of the emerging Green organizations and other non-governmental organizations that were going to raise environmental awareness, and she had actually established some of them herself. She was one of those talented people who lives without wasting a second, dividing their time hour by hour. I can never do that; I'm an unorganized, confused person, hah!"

She sighed. She had finished her coffee, and I still hadn't decided whether I should buy her another one.

"On that Christmas Eve, the doorbell rang and it was a man with a basket full of food and drink. Must be the wrong address, Fairy Tale said. But the address was right. The publisher of the poetry book had sent his poet a Christmas basket. Don't you find it surreal that there is such a publisher on Earth? I mean, is there a publisher who would send a gift to a poet who wrote a single book? But her name was Fairy Tale and she had a publisher characteristic of fairy tales. It's impossible to express to you our joy as we opened that basket. From the basket that we dove into with screams of hunger and glee, came smoked meat and fish, canned desserts, various cheeses, buns, chocolates, bags of coffee and a bottle of champagne. Can you imagine that? Just like in fairy tales . . . That Christmas was unforgettable even for someone like me who does not have a Christmas culture. We really had a good time. The children had prepared a puppet show for us. After they went to bed, we turned on the heat in the sauna, relaxed in there, and didn't sleep until the morning, sharing our plans and dreams. Oh, everybody in that Northern country has a sauna in their house or apartment, no matter how small it is. We made that night an unforgettable page in our lives. We had achieved this working together. Friendship, the feeling of sharing, and being motivated for life: these three make up a very special mix."

I bought her another coffee. I don't know if she understood that this was an extra. But I liked her story, half of which I sensed to be a fairy tale. The fiction was a little naive, a little amateurish, but surely I couldn't expect a traveler that I met on a train trip to be an expert short story writer or novelist.

"After a year, I left that Northern country and came back to my homeland in the Mediterranean. I always do that when I feel like taking refuge in a safe place. Then I set off again for unknown and stormy harbors . . ."

She stopped talking and looked around. She remembered that she was in the dining car of a train heading south. That's when she noticed her freshened coffee and perked up. I think she understood that the coffee had to do with the fact that I liked her travel story. She smiled, and I smiled back.

"At the end of the summer, my boyfriend who had left me came back. But as someone who spent that dark and long winter all alone, I felt that he fell short. I mean . . . you know, I had changed, I had grown up a little more, and he just wasn't enough for me; he was too small and narrow for me. No, no, it's not the feeling of revenge. Emptiness, nothingness . . . I don't know how to put it. I just didn't have any feelings, good or bad, for my ex-boyfriend. I'm sure you've experienced that, haven't you . . ."

The love part of the travel story must have been true, because as she was talking about that, the traces of what she had lived through during those days were revealed on her face. Love-pain is a pain that always stays fresh despite one's age and the time that has passed.

"As for Fairy Tale, she is now the Minister for the Environment in her country," she said.

Then she stood up slowly and went away, wishing me a nice trip. She hadn't finished her coffee. And I've never run into her again. Looking back on her, I concluded that she hadn't managed to end her story well. At least that's what I thought for years, until I went to Finland in the middle of 2000 and saw articles in the newspapers about the woman Minister for the Environment who rode her bicycle even to the Ministry, and who was greatly admired by her people. First I thought that it must have been a coincidence. But then when I discovered that the Minister was a tall, black-haired woman, I couldn't wait any longer; I asked her name. They said the name of the Minister for the Environment was Satu Hassi. And, yes, I asked the question: "What does Satu mean in Finnish?"

They said "Fairy Tale."

Fairy Tale.

But then who was that person who told me this story and what is she doing now?

Why Doesn't Santa Love Me, Daddy?

In fact, I'm not the right person to tell this story. We are served lives full of stories that are not right for us but that we have to go through nonetheless. Is that just? As if anyone on Earth ever witnessed divine justice . . . Or has it also escaped our memory that it was Boccaccio who, after sixty-five years, took Dante's famous work named simply *Commedia* and turned it into *Divina Commedia* by adding a single word? So I guess I am the narrator of this story for the reasons I just mentioned: because I am so not the right person.

It all started in a town in Turkey called Demre. Demre is a small paradise on the Mediterranean coast, part of the long coastline that stretches as far as the eye can see, where blue and green meet the generous sun that tints them red: the Turkish Riviera, as we Northern Europeans call it. But Demre's real significance stems from the belief that it is the place where Saint Nicholas, known as Noel Baba, Father Christmas, in Turkey, was born and passed away. I will have to remind those who ridicule this claim, wondering what on Earth the Saint Nicholas of Finnish origins, who glides over snow in a sleigh pulled by reindeers while chuckling merrily, is doing in a Muslim,

Mediterranean country, that the Finns are originally from Asia and thus are not Vikings, and that Islam didn't exist in Saint Nicholas' time. The Santa in Demre does not look at all like the white-bearded, fat, loud, Coca Cola-invented man that we have in Europe. Rather than a character from a fairy tale, the Anatolian Father Christmas, as depicted in a bronze statue given by the Russians to the Turks as a gift and standing now in the main square of Demre, looks more like a portly, even good-looking bishop: bearded, hooded, clad in robes, watching over the children clinging to the hems of his robes, with a modest bag hanging over his back. Well, that actually makes sense. As for the Turks, they established a Noel Baba Foundation long ago and recognized Saint Nicholas as an Anatolian saint with Lycian predecessors, on account of some theological and archeological references. However, I think what they are really interested in is the number of tourists that will visit the area and the foreign currency the tourists will spend there. Whatever, I have got nothing to do with this. I don't celebrate Christmas, and I am not a devout believer. But I suddenly found myself bang in the middle of a Christmas story even though I had wanted to escape anything related to Christmas during the holidays and therefore had specifically come to Turkey, where there was no Christmas and no celebration thereof.

Mine was a perfect flight. A flight from the consumption frenzy, political pollution, greed and hypocrisy . . . A brief flight from the embarrassment of being a citizen of one of the countries that occupied others and deprived them of freedom, all for the sake of "democracy." A flight from desperation, from the obligation to shave, and of course from myself. A breather . . . When we want an escape, we Europeans usually go for destinations that are unspoiled, cheap and exotic; and these places tend to have magnificent coasts on the Mediterranean or the oceans. Most Europeans no longer consider Turkey an exotic country with clichés like Ali Baba and the Forty Thieves or flying carpets in the harem, but (there is always a "but" in our minds, ready to be used in self-defense of our miserable souls!) it is a fascinating getaway country to find some peace of mind, and you can do this easily, as it is still affordable—even for someone like me who gets by on part-time jobs to avoid earning money from selling all of his time to others, and who prefers to read and write instead. When I decided to use the Christmas and New Year's break to escape and hide somewhere far away from family dinners, the shopping frenzy infesting all the streets of the Christian world, the noise and the crowds, I went to Antalya on a friend's recommendation. I checked into a hotel and rented a motorbike. I went swimming in the morning, explored surrounding towns by motorbike after breakfast, and came back in the evening. I enjoyed being free from the obligation to shave and, thanks to not knowing the language, from the meaningless small talk that suffocates my soul and that is universal no matter where you go. And in the remaining time, I read and took notes for the book I was going to write before I died. Everything was absolutely perfect. I left everybody alone and in return they left me alone.

On December 26, thrilled to have quietly escaped the Christmas consumption monster, I ventured outside Antalya, found excuses to get as far as Demre, and once there, visited the ancient church of Saint Nicholas of Demre, which serves as a museum today. It was cool but sunny. I swam for a while. Then, while I was sitting in a coffeehouse enjoying the Turkish black tea I like so much and which they refer to as "rabbit's blood," curiously associating the color of this delicious tea with that of blood, I saw the child. A skinny girl, about six years old, in a blue tracksuit, was standing in front of the statue of Saint Nicholas in the center of the garden, shouting at him angrily and crying. She was shouting angrily at the Saint Nicholas statue, her short black hair pulled up into a ponytail that looked like a fountain, shedding tears from her huge jet-black eyes that looked like those of a Japanese anime character, covering almost all of her unhealthy-looking face. I had never witnessed a scene like this before and was genuinely shocked. What was going on? Before I knew it, I was standing next to the little girl. I was dying to find out what a child so obviously poor and raised in a culture without Christmas wanted from Santa. When she saw me, the child was first taken aback, utterly petrified; then her face went pale with fear as if she had seen a ghost and she stopped crying; her tears froze on her cheeks and she eyed me fearfully. When I saw that she was scared, I drew back. We both stood there for a while, eyes locked, without saying a word. Then she muttered something delirious, and then, as though I had done something terrible to her, she started crying and yelling at me; but I couldn't make out a single word. Never in my wildest dreams could I have imagined that I would be this sorry for not knowing Turkish. Just then, a small-built man in uniform I had not seen coming darted forward, grabbed the girl by the ear and pulled her, almost dragging her. The child was still talking to me while she continued to cry. I had no idea what kind of trouble I was getting myself into when I told the man to leave the child alone in my own language. That small-built, frail man of about thiry-five in his oversized uniform shot me such a fierce look that I knew he did not fear me at all despite the fact that I was much taller and better built than he was. At that very moment, the child escaped his grip, ran to me and, holding onto my leg, said something to me in a beseeching tone. The man, who I would find out later was Mehmet the Warden, the warden of the ancient church of Saint Nicholas and the father of the girl, reached out with a swift move, grabbed the girl by the arm and, literally scraping her off me, took her away. As I did not know then that the man was the girl's father, I thought he had abducted her.

And, even if he was her father, what he did was an act of violence. Had this happened in Europe, I could have saved the girl, filing complaints about Mehmet for having hurt his child; but we were in Turkey and all those people watching us continued to sip their "rabbit's blood" tea as if everything was absolutely normal. Just like everywhere I had been to, the people in this small town I had taken refuge in to get away from other people had not failed to upset me in a very bad way.

I should have forgotten her. As someone who had never married and stayed away on his own free will and intention from the prison called family, away from children who were a fertile breeding ground for human defects, and from the voice of religions, which ostracized those who did not belong to them, turning them into "the other," I should have forgotten that child immediately. However, while I was sitting at my table set against a wonderful view of the Mediterranean, with a selection of scrumptious Turkish dishes in front of me, enjoying a glass of high quality Turkish red wine made of Öküzgözü grapes, I suddenly remembered the poor girl with the huge black eyes crying in front of the statue of Saint Nicholas, and how she was dragged away with fury by her father, and with that, I lost all joy in the evening. To top it all, that night I had a dream of her talking to me in Turkish and crying again. It was a terrible night. Early in the morning, I went to the tourism agency in Antalya. I found a young man working there who could speak my language, put him in a cab with me and set off. My sole desire was to understand what that child was asking me!

Though I didn't really have the luxury of visiting the same place twice during my short, ten-day winter holiday, here I was heading back to the town where the Santa who I was running away from was allegedly born. We were talking about divine justice, right? The young man, who was going to be my interpreter, was sitting in the front seat of the car I had arranged to take us to Demre. He was the son of a

Turkish migrant family in Europe, and my mother tongue was one of his too. However, because he felt like an outcast in the country where he was born and was a citizen, he had left there and settled in Turkey. Throughout the journey, he told me about some of the acts of racist violence he experienced, in such a calm manner you would think they happened to someone else, in the city where we both were born and lived in different years. As he did so, I sought refuge in my habitual dream of a world without human beings—a wonderful paradise consisting of plants and animals only.

When we reached Demre and looked for Mehmet, the warden of the church, we learned that he was on leave that day because he had to take his daughter Meryem to the hospital, as she had suddenly fallen ill during the night. My interpreter told me that the name Meryem was the Turkish version of Mary and cracked a joke that he thought was divine: Holy Mary and Saint Nicholas! Of course, I did not give up and go back to my hotel. Instead, as you might have guessed, I went to the small public hospital of Demre, along with my interpreter, because by now I had irrevocably become part of this story and had no choice but take it to the very end. On a bench in the hospital garden, I saw Mehmet the Warden sitting with a young woman in a cheap nylon headscarf, long skirt and worn-out cardigan, grieving. This Mehmet, wearing jeans and a denim jacket of a brand widely copied in Turkey, sitting there sad and quiet, looked younger and more innocent to me and did not fit the role of the evil father figure who inflicted violence upon his little daughter the day before. As I was standing there watching him, he turned his head suddenly, saw me and and clearly recognized me. I thought he might attack and waited, my feet planted firmly on the ground. Instead, Mehmet jumped up from the bench, came toward me shyly, smiling with an expression of great gratitude, and reached out to shake my hand vigorously. People who saw us could easily have concluded we were old friends. Holding his blood-shot eyes on me, he said something. "He thanks you for coming to visit his daughter," said my interpreter. I was disappointed but didn't show it; I just nodded. He, on the other hand, started to speak rapidly in a concerned voice. First, I waited, assuming that he would eventually tire and take a break, but he wouldn't stop talking. He talked so much that I finally could not wait anymore and had to stop him by waving my hand and asking the interpreter what he was saying. The child had come down with a cold while she was waiting for days in front of the statue of Saint Nicholas, and they had brought her to the hospital when she became feverish and delirious the night before. I was told that the young woman with the headscarf, who was still sitting on the bench like a shadow, silent, her eyes cast sadly toward the ground, was Meryem's mother. In Mehmet, who had welcomed me cheerfully, as if I had discovered and brought a cure that would make his daughter better, I now saw a compassionate father loving his child dearly, and I got confused because I couldn't figure out which one was his genuine self. My scrutinizing gaze was fixed on him as he guided the interpreter and me, nudging us towards the hospital building. The hospital looked like a small, clean and old-fashioned clinic. Once inside, he introduced me to the doctor and the nurse with such enthusiasm that one might think I was a close relative of Meryem's. The female doctor of the small hospital was looking at me curiously, wondering why a European tourist had interrupted his vacation and visited the hospital to ask about the health of a child he had only seen once. Her admiring gaze unmistakably read "so, humanity is not dead yet," no matter the language. To be honest, I was there only because I was burning to find out what the child had asked me, but now I had swerved to a point where I no longer dared say this, which made me feel uncomfortable.

Fortunately, the moment did not last long. The doctor had forbidden visits because of the child's high fever, so I literally ran out of the hospital and into the garden. Back there, Mehmet the Warden started to talk rapid-fire again. Either he was raving like that because of his sorrow, or he believed that his sorrow would subside if he talked like that. What I could get from the interpreted summary was that Mehmet the Warden, who was trying to provide for his seven children on a minimum wage, had been in trouble for quite some time with his youngest daughter Meryem, who, he complained, was living in a fantasy world. Mehmet, who was a devout Muslim, considered it a sin to accept the existence of Saint Nicholas, who was the first bishop of the museum-church he was watching for a living. However, foreigners who had bought houses and settled in Antalya in recent years dressed up as Santa for Christmas and distributed presents to make the children in their community happy, which caused little Meryem, who was already a dreamer, to completely "go astray."

"No matter how many times I tell her that there is no Santa in our religion, she just won't get it, because she's still a child! But then I saw that she was genuinely sad, so much so that she wouldn't eat anymore . . . Her mother and I, we pinched and scraped to buy her a plastic doll for our Ramadan feast, but she wouldn't even touch it, and insisted on a present from Santa, crying, 'Why doesn't Santa love me, Daddy?' We tried to explain to her that Saint Nicholas was not a saint of Muslim children, but, alas, she just wouldn't understand . . ." Just as it was crossing my mind that bigotry is a bad thing, Mehmet added, "Sir, honestly, what would you do if your children wanted to jump over a bonfire for our Hidirellez spring festival celebrating the prophet Al-Khidr?" What could I do? I was dumbstruck.

After this encounter, Mehmet the Warden came to visit me at the hotel every evening of the remaining days I spent in Antalya. Every evening after work, he would travel 140 kilometers from Demre on a minibus, wait for me in the lobby and then update me on Meryem's condition with the help of the hotel staff who would translate for him. Meryem was still in the hospital trying to recover from severe pneumonia. At first, I did not protest and let him keep up his act, but on the last day of my holiday, the evening before I was to leave for my cold and dark city and my lonely, quiet home, I couldn't take it any longer and told him in a firm voice that I was not rich and that he should not expect any material gains from me. When he heard the translation, Mehmet the Warden swayed as if slapped in the face, melted and shrank. He was so offended and hurt by what I had said that he was close to tears. When I saw his reaction, I was terribly embarrassed and understood right away that, actually, he wasn't expecting anything material from me; I believed that with all my heart. What did he want from me then? It seemed that Turkish people, unlike us, preferred not to talk openly about their soft spots like love, pain, sorrow and money. Maybe that's why they were so boisterous in celebrating their heroes.

"Sir, may God be pleased with you, you concerned yourself with our daughter and raised our spirits. It is true that I will ask something of you, but I swear to God, it has got nothing to do with money, no! Oh sir, for the love of God, tell my crazy daughter Meryem that you are not Santa before you leave. I'm at your mercy!" Once he pulled himself together, Mehmet's words came out with pride, and I first thought there was a mistranslation, but that had never been an issue with this young man from the reception who had interpreted for me before. Then it was my turn to be taken aback. As someone who had fled to a country without Christmas just to get away from everything related to it, I thought Santa was the last person I could transform into, and yet it seemed I had become him! Frustrated, I asked Mehmet what the hell he was talking about. "Don't you ever look into the mirror, sir? You stand there, right in front of my dreamer girl, almost an identical reproduction of our statue in Demre, wearing that same Saint Nicholas hat, your beard just like his, and now, I swear to God, this stubborn girl will refuse to accept that Saint Nicholas doesn't exist, to save her life!" Mehmet pleaded desperately. I paused and thought about the statue. Yes, Mehmet was right. Tall and well-built, that statue man did indeed resemble me as much as a brother would. Or rather, I resembled him . . . Then I remembered my beard that had slightly grown as I hadn't been shaving and how it had started to go gray now that I was in my forties . . . And then the hood I had covered my wet hair with because I had just come out of the sea . . . Goddamn it! Now I see . . . But it would never have crossed my mind . . . Yes, it was true, I could very well have looked like Saint Nicholas of Demre in the flesh through little Meryem's eyes.

It was New Year's Eve and the lobby and restaurant of the hotel I was staying at were decorated for the New Year, which the Turks had been celebrating for eighty years as if it were Christmas. Colorful ribbons and lanterns had been hung up everywhere and there was even a gigantic plastic Christmas tree in the middle of the lobby. Though unbelievable, it was true that even if the date shifted seven days, there was probably nowhere left on Earth to escape this Christmas craze! As I was staring at those decorations, vexed, I heard Mehmet say something to the receptionist in a harsh and angry tone so unlike that sincere, loving, sad fatherly voice that killed me while he was talking about little Meryem. I hadn't been able to get used to these sudden changes in him, so I was wondering what he said, and asked. "He said, 'See, God Almighty's act! This year, New Year's Eve and the Feast of Sacrifice coincide.* Now some reckless, sinful Turks will supposedly have fun, drinking and dancing here until the wee hours and then

attend early morning prayers, for heaven's sake!'" said the receptionist in a dull voice. When I asked "Is tomorrow an Islamic feast?" in
surprise, they both nodded. Was that so? I said "Great!" icily. I had an
idea. Mehmet the Warden couldn't possibly be so strict or heartless
as to turn down a Santa bringing a present for his sick daughter on an
Islamic holy day. Besides, I was not the one responsible for the Islamic
Feast of Sacrifice coinciding with these Christmas-like festivities that
the Turks identified with New Year's.

Three hours prior to the departure of my plane, I was back in the
hospital where Meryem stayed, with presents consisting of a box
of chocolates and my expensive waterproof watch. The female doctor recognized me and epxlained to me in her broken English that
Meryem's condition was still serious and that they were going to
transfer her to another, better equipped hospital in Ankara. It broke
my heart that the life of the only child on Earth who believed I was
Santa Claus was in danger. When I finally got the permission to just
pop my head into the room, I saw Meryem, who just a few days before
was clinging to my leg, crying and asking me for a toy, looking even
smaller in her bed now and sleeping as if unconscious. To humor her,
I had kept the beard that I had intended to shave at the end of my
vacation. I stuck my bearded and hooded head further into the room
and called out to her the sentence I had practiced umpteen times
throughout the evening: *"Meryeem, Merhaba Meryem! Bak Noel Baba
Bayramı bugün!"*** But she did not stir. I waited a little then repeated
the same sentence several times. No, there was no movement at all.
Tiptoeing, I went to her side. I left the watch and chocolates on her
bedside table. I looked at her pale little face. "Meryeem, Merhaba

---

* As the date of the four-day Feast of Sacrifice is set in the Islamic lunar calendar, it shifts back ten to
eleven days each year in the Gregorian (Christian) calendar.

** "Meryem, hellooo, Meryem! Look, it's Santa Day today!"

Meryem! Bak Noel Baba Bayramı bugün!" I whispered. The child was unconscious. She still did not stir. I was angry with myself. What was I doing there and what was I expecting? I still had not learned my lesson! I stayed there a while longer and listened to the regular breathing of the young girl. Just when I was about to leave, the child suddenly opened her eyes, looked at me and smiled. Really. Meryem looked at me and smiled. Then she closed her eyes again.

For the life of me, I would never have imagined that I would be happy because of the smile of a little girl I did not know, but I was—I was genuinely happy! When my plane took off and I realized that I was watching Antalya become smaller under me with almost sentimental feelings, I understood that that smile still hanging ridiculously on my face was Meryem's. At that moment, I already knew I would come back to Antalya. If Meryem persevered and survived, I could visit her again next Christmas in Demre. Of course I would . . . I took out the piece of paper on which Mehmet the Warden had written his phone number, unfolded it and looked at it. Then I put it back into my pocket with care, as if it held Meryem's smile.

To Ingo Arend

My thanks to Prof. Nevzat Çevik, Head of the Department of Archeology, Akdeniz University, for the information he provided on Demre/Myra and St. Nicholas.

Dr. John E. Liho and the Plane to Honolulu

"I would never have imagined that a dream could save a human life."

Hawaiian American doctor John E. Liho, who was sitting next to me on the plane to Honolulu, was not someone who liked to chat with strangers on trips. I too am fastidious when it comes to friendships, including those that start on journeys. But Dr. John E. Liho was, in his own words, returning from "mainland" America to "homeland" Hawaii after many years and was under enormous emotional pressure when he shared this eerie information on dreams with me—someone who happened to be there by sheer coincidence. If instead of me, someone who wasn't interested in dreams or human lives had been sitting there, perhaps that person would not have listened to Dr. John E. Liho's strange story, which I am going to tell here in a moment. And if like me, you think that dreams are the most uncensored synopses of our subconscious contradictions, and some dreams are like individual short art films, you too would not believe that a dream could save a human life. In fact I have to admit, not one of my dreams has saved a single life yet, and probably never will; but from now on, my share will be to tell the story, if there is one, of dreams and lives.

To be honest, when I boarded the plane to Honolulu, I was a mess, with my head aching cruelly, sinusitis blocking my face mercilessly as in every winter, an impertinent cold that had confined me to bed the previous week persisting. Talking to the passenger sitting next to me throughout the four-hour flight from Houston to Honolulu was number one on my "Top Three Least Desired Things To Do in Life" list at that moment. I just wanted to sleep and be bright-eyed and bushy-tailed when I landed in Hawaii so I could accomplish a lot in a short time as the first person in the family in six hundred years (to the best of my knowledge) to step on any one of the Polynesian Islands in the Pacific Ocean. Once I arrived, instead of falling fast asleep in my hotel room in Honolulu, I wanted to see a myriad of sites, from legendary Waikiki Beach to the Missouri Memorial at Pearl Harbor; from the island's magnificent landscape, which also served as the setting for *Jurassic Park*, to its sunset, said to be unrivalled in the world for its beauty. However, my plan failed and I couldn't sleep on the plane. My seatmate hit me in my soft spot, so much so that when I landed in Honolulu, not only was I deprived of sleep, but I was so stunned, so overstimulated and restless as if from too much caffeine, that I would not be able to sleep for several days.

"It was like a slap in my face when I learned that dreams could save human lives, and everything has changed since."

No stranger you happen to sit next to on a plane will simply blurt out such a statement, and neither did Dr. John E. Liho. Liho. Before he had me all ears with this sentence, he followed all rules of etiquette characteristic of frequent travelers. First, he greeted me with a cool smile, and we exchanged bon voyages borrowed from French. Then, he bent down and moved my backpack which I had tucked away under the seat in front of me a little to the side to avoid touching it with his feet. He even offered me chewing gum he produced from his pocket, to prevent the pressure from plugging my ears during takeoff. Next, he took out the *USA Today* he had placed in the seat-back pocket in front of him and began reading it. Back then, I was living in New York with my small family consisting of my son and his father. My son was eight years old and in third grade at a school in Manhattan. I was researching Ottoman and British archives in the New York Public Library, one of the most beautiful libraries in the world, for my novel *The Long White Cloud–Gallipoli*, which I was writing at the time. And my then husband, the father of my son, was trying to promote his new animated feature film for children to the international art film market. A few days before I was sitting next to Dr. John E. Liho on the plane, my son's school holiday had started. As it was winter in the northern hemisphere and New York was cold and gloomy, I was suffering from sinusitis and almost bursting because of breathlessness. All three of us wanted to be in Istanbul during the two-week holiday break, but even iterating the cost of a holiday in Istanbul was intimidating. And then, in an ad in the Travel section of the *New York Times*, we saw that for the price of one New York–Istanbul ticket, the three of us could spend five days in Hawaii, where it was always summer and the temperature never dropped below 75 degrees. And so here we were, on the plane to Honolulu on the nearest available date.

Although the three of us sat together on the plane from New York to Houston, we could not arrange the same seating order on our connecting flight to Honolulu. So I took advantage of this mishap, seated my son next to his father, and made plans to sleep in peace in an aisle seat two rows in front of them. The window seat that was my favorite as a child seems claustrophobic to me now that I am an adult and I always go for the aisle seat. I needed that sleep on the plane so desperately that I took painkilling and sleep-inducing nighttime medicine even before I boarded and kept my sleep mask at the ready so as not to be disturbed by the light. All I wanted was a little sleep. Everything was set. I turned around slowly, smiled at my son and husband, and whispered "Sweet dreams to me," but I didn't know yet that John E. Liho, who had personally witnessed how a dream could save a human life, was sitting next to me.

"I have two sons and a daughter," he said. He had probably noticed me turning around and smiling to my family every now and then since I had gotten on the plane. I smiled at him reluctantly. "Kids are great, but people should only have kids if they have enough time for them!" he continued. I mustered another reluctant smile. "Unfortunately, in the prime of their life when people can have kids, they don't have time for them." I pretended to have not heard that last sentence, because it was weightier than the other two, and I wanted to sleep. I was fiddling with my sleep mask, about to put it on, trying not to be rude to my seatmate, when he said in a very soft, calm voice, "If a dream could save a human life, there should be other things that I can save still." I remember freezing for a moment, my sleep mask in my hand. When I recovered from the initial shock these words had induced in me, my first thought was that I had misunderstood him. But my seatmate was speaking perfect American English. Then I tried to chalk it up to my being drowsy, but I had heard every single word in his sentence. When he noticed that I was scrutinizing him, he turned to me and said, "I would never have imagined that a dream could save a human life." The plane had taken off and the fuse had been lit: I was curious now.

"Will this be your first time in Hawaii?" he then asked—as if I wanted to talk about anything other than his dream. Besides, his question was ironic for me, knowing that throughout history, Turks have traveled almost exclusively to migrate and that my visit to Hawaii for touristic purposes was a kind of miracle; but at that moment, Dr. John E. Liho did not yet know where I was from.

"Oh, the first time you go there, they bother you with lots of touristic stuff. You will have to 'Aloha' everyone and 'Mahalo' for each thank you. There is also this 'Hang loose' thing which you really can't avoid!" he said, raising his right hand, extending his thumb and little finger while curling the three middle fingers and pressing them into his palm. This resembled the *bozkurt*, the wolf's head-like hand gesture of a nationalist group in Turkey, but Dr. John E. Liho knew nothing of that. "This gesture represents one of the Hawaiian philosophies that advises one to take it easy, to relax," he added. To be honest, I was not intending to sacrifice my precious sleep to learn about Hawaiian philosophical gestures, and I urgently had to find a way to skip these and to start talking about how dreams saved lives. So, I eyed him carefully and introduced myself formally. I told him briefly that I was a writer from Istanbul living in New York. In return, my elegant seatmate, who was in his forties, of average height, good-looking, wearing clothes that suggested both wealth and good taste, introduced himself formally to me. He was a heart surgeon living in Houston with his wife and three children. He had studied at the University of Texas, liked baseball and golf, and did outdoor sports during their family holidays in their cottage. Later in our conversation, he would show me on his mobile phone a picture of his white American wife, who was striking in her ostentatious pose and as beautiful as a model, and his three very cute children. As he didn't mention any details about his Hawaiian background when describing his life, I assumed he was born on the mainland as a mixed Hawaiian *hapa*. But, frankly, I was not at all interested in Dr. John E. Liho's seemingly perfect white American family life. Rather, I was determined not to leave the plane without uncovering this dream story for which I had sacrificed my sleep. Hoping that a cliché would tease him and ensure we got down to business, I said, "I believe for a positive scientist like yourself to become interested in the metaphysical aspect of dreams, you must have gone through a significant experience." "Believe me, I have," he said, smiling bitterly. "But I bet it's nothing like one day you had a dream and your life changed!" I ventured my ironic second sentence. Now the ball was in his court.

"Maybe you are not going to believe me, but it was exactly like that. Two weeks ago, I had a dream. First I dismissed it as an ordinary dream, but its impact was very extensive . . . I couldn't pull myself together . . ." he said and then stopped. As his silence continued, I lost interest; maybe his story wasn't as intriguing as I had assumed it would be. How could someone with such a planned and polished life have any interesting dreams left anyway? How could I possibly summon the sleep I had pointlessly lost and get a little, just a little of it?

"I had a dream of a childhood friend of mine who I had not seen, called or mentioned in name in twenty years. He was shouting 'Call me, save me, Ekela!' and crying. He was still a child, but I was my adult self, in a white operating gown, ready to enter the operating room. He was tugging at my gown and begging. 'Duke, why have you still not grown up?' I was asking him while looking at him in amazement. Then a huge wave came and inundated Duke Mokae. The final image was Duke's child-sized hand, and the last thing I heard was his cry: 'Save me, Ekela!' I woke up in a pool of sweat, thought I'd had a nightmare because I had eaten too much, and decided not to tell anyone, not even my wife, about this dream. I forgot, or rather chose to forget, the dream during my busy schedule the following day. However, when I had the same dream the next night, I understood that I would not be able to escape it. You understand when you can't escape something, did you know that?"

That was not a bad start at all, yet it lacked the essential spark that would increase the value of this dream and turn it into a real story. But at least I had learned now that Dr. Liho, who introduced himself to me as John, actually had one more name: Ekela. This proved that there was not much use of titles in dreams, even if they were scientific; there was this real side of dreams.

"As a matter of fact, that Duke in my dream wasn't just a childhood friend," Dr. Ekela Liho added.

You know how you feel relieved and freed of a secret that's been burning in you once you reveal it to someone, preferably someone distant and alien who you will never see again? It is with exactly that sense of relief that Dr. Liho appeared to exhale all the air within him. But when I glanced discretely at his face, careful not to rattle him, he did not look relieved to me at all. On the contrary, he was frowning and his face had gone pale; he looked concerned. Meanwhile, the crew had started to serve non-alcoholic beverages, and though I thought Dr. Liho might benefit from a strong drink, we were in economy class, so we were left to sip only our cups of orange juice.

"I began to think that Duke was there not only as my friend, but also as my past that I had abandoned altogether, because I found myself reminiscing often about my childhood in Honolulu."

I then pictured him as a very smart and good-looking young man itching to climb the social ladder, leaving behind not only his childhood friend Duke, but many other pieces of his past in order to live that wealthy white American family life. The bright, bold and very determined Ekela Liho!

"Did you call Duke?" I asked softly.

"I couldn't. It's difficult to know how to call someone you haven't spoken to in twenty tears. You don't even know if he's still alive."

Wow, I said to myself. Is it really worth it to climb so far that you do not even know whether your closest friend from childhood is alive? To pay such a high price just for the sake of recreating yourself from scratch? But then when I tried to think of how many people I knew over forty who were still in contact with their childhood friends, it was a painful thought. Even more painful when I thought of how some of them were conformists not bothered about the world as it is today, let alone their pasts. But this wasn't a good time for contemplation; I had to come up with something quickly that would encourage Dr. Liho to finish his story.

"My best friend in university, Müge, and I drifted apart too, and unfortunately we saw it coming . . ." I said, sighing woefully and thinking that I missed Müge even though we were living in the same city.

"But I started a search for him. Although I was very busy and preparations for my wife's birthday were well underway, I had people search for Duke. I even rallied the woman who works as a receptionist at our hospital. But the person who eventually managed to trace him was my brother who lives in Honolulu."

Writing this story now, I remember how difficult life was not too long ago without the search engine Google or the virtual detective Facebook, and I am both sad and glad that technological addictions are stronger than those for nicotine or caffeine.

"In fact, the first person I shocked was my brother, who was hearing my voice on the phone after so many years. When I asked him to find Duke's phone number, he couldn't believe his ears—not because I was asking about Duke, but because he was surprised I was calling him of all people, do you understand? I had already begun to regret calling him, when my mother seized the phone from him and asked if it was really her elder son Ekela talking. She always makes me feel guilty!"

Just as it was crossing my mind—Whose mother doesn't?—my son who was sitting two rows behind me came up to me and whispered into my ear, "Why don't you stop chatting and sleep, Mom! You know if you don't, you'll spoil our whole vacation!" and then returned to his seat next to his father. Sometimes the precision of timing can hurt. Not knowing what my son had whispered to me, Dr. John Ekela Liho said in a voice filled with longing, "The mother and son relationship in childhood is so strong and fascinating . . ."

"Well, were you able to find Duke?" I asked, as though in a hurry to sweep mother and son relationships under the rug.

"I did, five days ago," he said calmly.

Then he went silent. As his silence drew out, I started to make up alternative stories, but none was as enticing as the reality itself. The flight attendants had already emerged in the aisle with their carts and started to serve food. Dr. Liho, who helped me open the tray in front of me, said:

"When I called Duke, his son answered. Since he became a father at an early age, his son is seventeen years old. Before I could even finish saying my name to introduce myself, this young man politely interrupted me to say that his father talked about me frequently and was proud of me, and that he himself knew all our childhood memories. Can you imagine? While my own children know almost nothing about their father's life in Honolulu, Duke has been telling his children about me . . ."

And you say it is your mother who makes you feel guilty, oh, good-looking Dr. Ekela from Honolulu! I thought but managed to keep it to myself. Dr. Liho, who was asking the flight attendant serving us whether they had mahi-mahi fish, said to me in excitement, "All the fish you get in Hawaii is superb, but you can't leave the island without trying mahi-mahi." The expression on his face was like that of a child talking about his favorite toy, which made him look even more attractive. As there was no fish on the menu, we decided to take the chicken dish and made some obligatory remarks on the artificial the taste of airplane food, again signaling that we were both frequent travelers.

"And could you learn anything from Duke's son about his father that corresponded to your dream?" I asked, crunching on the salad in my mouth like a grazing sheep.

"As I was talking to his son, Duke came home, and when he found out that his son was on the phone with me, he grabbed it, and just like my mother, he couldn't believe that it was me. 'Ekela, Ekela, is it really you, brother?' he asked several times. He couldn't believe that I was calling him after twenty years, so I sang a few lines of a song called *Holoholo Ka'a* that we used to play on the ukulele. Then, weeping, he joined me in the song. It's a children's song which means 'You and I on a joy ride' in Hawaiian. While Duke was singing the song in tears on the phone, what disturbed me wasn't really his crying, but rather the fact that he might be embarrassed in front of his son. So I asked him whether I should call at another time. But he refused that vehemently. Maybe he was afraid that I would disappear for another twenty years. Then, without covering the receiver, he told his son to leave the room since he wanted to speak to me in private. His son must have left, because right after that he said to me, 'Ekela, I had decided to commit suicide tonight!'"

I only realized that I was shouting "No way!" in Turkish when I recognized my own voice. I am not sure whether Dr. Liho, who looked numb and in a trance-like state at that moment, had heard me, but my son came up to my row and nudged me, which meant "Pull yourself together!" As a mother who hadn't slept as planned during the trip and was therefore going to be grumpy during the vacation, and who couldn't help talking to the male stranger sitting next to her and crying out "No way," I was probably not the ideal role model for an eight-year-old child. That was never my goal in life anyway, but once you are a mother, you want your child to really, truly admire everything you do!

Unaware of the mother-and-son drama that I just experienced, and looking at a point in the distance while chewing his food delicately, Dr. Liho continued, "I said to him, 'Duke, I dreamed about you twice last week. In both dreams, you were repeatedly asking me to call you. However, I wouldn't want to interfere with the decision of an adult . . ."

I almost couldn't hold back my second "No way!" Was this really something a person who had taken the Hippocratic Oath would say?

"But . . . there must be a reason I had this dream twice. I'll come to visit you next week in Honolulu. 'Would you mind delaying the execution of your decision until then?' I asked him."

Because I did not know whether he was joking, I turned to face him, with my lips pursed tightly so as not to laugh, but I am afraid Dr. Liho was serious.

"This is why I am on the plane right now," he said and asked the flight attendant who was passing for a cup of coffee. I breathed a sigh of relief so deep that one of my sinuses that had been clogged for days popped open and I was able breathe through my nose. For people who suffer from sinusitis, this is as miraculous as going to heaven! The food service was still continuing and Dr. Liho, who had not finished his food, was asking for more and more coffee. I knew that I would never be able to find out whether he did this because he had lost his appetite or because wanted to stay in shape. But I had a feeling that there were some points still missing in this story and I wanted to get to them before the plane landed in Honolulu. I wanted for my trip to the island to include this delicious memory whose taste would linger in my mouth for a long time.

"If Hawaii is as beautiful as in the pictures and movies, it shouldn't be so easy to live in Texas after that," I said with a final effort. "Especially for someone like you who has spent his childhood here . . ."

"You are right, Hawaii is very beautiful indeed. Clichés such as 'Hawaii, the pearl of the Pacific Ocean' do not suffice to describe its tropical forests and golden sandy beaches, its cuisine, which you will find exotic, its music and dance. The lei, the necklace of flowers they are going to hang around your neck when you get off the plane, and the hula dance performed with grass skirts: these are not the cheap touristic tokens they are taken for. They are genuine expressions of affection, love and freedom for Hawaiians."

Just as I was thinking that Duke had entered Dr. Liho's dreams at the right time, based not on what he was telling me, but on his voice, which was infused with longing and pride as he was telling me these things, he continued:

"Yes, I could say that I felt very lonely and alien, especially in my first years on the mainland, but only exiles would understand what I mean. Perhaps mine was voluntary, but isn't the life an exile leads, suspended between where he was born and raised and where he has to live, a life that is double and restless?" he said and then asked a flight attendant for more coffee.

"I agree with you to a certain extent, but I'm not sure whether a journey taken without a threat of death or torture could be considered exile . . . Of course, I don't want to be unfair to you, but . . ." I mumbled.

"Ah, madam, believe me, when you realize that you are actually outside of that circle that you seemed to be in, you experience an identity shock that is nothing short of torture! And if you are very young when that happens, you might do anything, literally anything, because you panic!" said Dr. Liho. Probably worried that he had sounded harsh, he softened his tone and asked, "Do you know where Duke got his name?" Before I could reply in the negative, he said, "The namesake of my friend Duke is Duke Paoa Kahanamoku, who was of aboriginal descent, a completely indigenous, great Hawaiian athlete. He won two gold medals and one silver medal in swimming at the Olympics. This great athlete, whose statue you will see on Waikiki Beach, was also a pioneer in introducing surfing, a Hawaiian invention, to the world. He, on his part, got his name from the Duke of Edinburgh, who visited Honolulu many years ago. Are you following me?"

"Like your name is John Ekela?" I replied hesitantly. In response to that, he leaned forward slightly, took out an elegant wallet from his back pocket and offered me the business card he withdrew from it. I looked at the card that read *Dr. John E. Liho – Heart Surgeon* on top of an address, email address and office phone numbers.

"Ekela means 'help' in the Hawaiian language. Help is a very important and sacred concept in our culture. The Polynesian people, who are descendants of peoples who have been living happily for eight hundred years thousands of miles away from the mainland, regard it as an honorable tradition to commit suicide rather than surrender to strangers," he said with the air of an anthropologist lecturing his pupil. "Hawaii was the last state to join the United States in 1959."

"Are you implying then that you discovered a hint behind Duke's, your friend Duke's suicidal ideation related to surrender? Depressive feelings like defeat, failure, despair . . . I'm sorry, your dream has affected me so deeply that I think I can't follow you."

"I believe you have followed me very well," he said, smiling. "I don't know about that yet, but considering that I had a dream that has saved his life for at least fourteen days so far, I am hoping that perhaps the same could be true for my own life. Because I guess it's time my children met their grandmother and other relatives, and more importantly, their father's culture."

So *your* exile is coming to an end, I said only to myself, as I thought that it would be too much for Dr. Liho to hear now, especially from a stranger like me.

"But I decided that I should first come alone, talk to Duke one-on-one, and catch up with my mother and family who I have neglected for years. Getting my wife's support was the most pleasant surprise, believe me."

I remember smiling broadly despite my exhaustion and the pain that still blocked my face, defying the painkiller. Pain is temporary, but a good story can live forever and save lives. At that moment, Dr. Liho turned and looked at me. He broke into a smile too.

"The Turks I know always say to me, 'We Turks do not like traveling,' but the two Turkish doctors who work in our hospital seize any opportunity they can to take their own families to Turkey to see their extended families. Okay, maybe they don't go and discover Europe or Hawaii, but they take their children who were born in the States to the country where they themselves were born and don't neglect their own culture . . ." Then he squinted and examined my face with the scrutiny of a doctor and asked, "Could you possibly have a migraine?" Laughing, I told him about my sinusitis, my splitting headache, and how I had planned to sleep on this trip.

"Oh, don't worry, the moment you land in Honolulu, you will have no trace of any disease!" he said with jovial pride. "Hawaii's air, water and food are so fresh and healthful, they are said to cure all known ailments. Among the grandmothers and grandfathers in my family, there are many who have reached the age of one hundred and still enjoy a quality life. Hawaii has the longest life expectancy of any state in the US anyway. Remember, hang loose!" he said while making the hang loose gesture.

These words raised my hopes that I would not suffer from sinusitis or sleep deprivation in Honolulu. In fact, during the five days we spent there, all three of us were healthy and content.

When the plane began its descent to land, I wanted to confide a very private emotion I had during this four-hour flight talking to Dr. Liho, who I would not have a chance to see again. I wanted to tell him, "Dr. Liho, or Ekela, if you would allow me to call you Ekela, would you do me a favor? Please, find a way to have another dream that will make Duke choose life," but I couldn't bring myself to say it. When we were leaving the plane, we shook hands and looked at each other meaningfully like two strangers who had shared a vital secret, and then we wished one another luck. Aloha, Ekela!

I haven't seen Dr. John Ekela Liho again. I haven't tried to contact him from the addresses or phone numbers on the business card he gave me. I haven't Googled him for a new contact address or more information only a click away. Because some secrets need to remain secrets so that they can fly forever in the miraculous skies of literature! But whenever I hear a Hawaiian tune, read something about the now very Americanized Polynesian culture, or hear a word that reminds me of mahi-mahi fish, which is indeed very tasty, I always catch myself wondering whether Duke is still alive and whether a dream can save a human life for more than fourteen days. Always.